Baba Yaga

Baba Yaga

Bratva Assassin Duet
Book One

Sarah Jane

Copyright © 2023 by Sarah Jane

All rights reserved.

No part of this book may be reproduced in any form or by any electronic or mechanical means, including information storage and retrieval systems, without written permission from the author, except for the use of brief quotations in a book review.

Warning: the unauthorized reproduction or distribution of this copyrighted work is illegal. Criminal copyright infringement, including infringement without monetary gain, is investigated by the FBI and is punishable by up to five years in prison and a fine of $250,000.

This is a work of fiction. Names, places, characters and incidents are either the product of the author's imagination or are used fictitiously, and any resemblance to any actual persons, living or dead, organizations, events or locales is entirely coincidental.

Song titles, businesses, products, apps, and social medias mentioned in this book are under the fair use law. Under no circumstance does the author claim any copyright of the those listed under fair use.

Edited by Jeanine Harrell

Cover by Black Widow Designs

Chapter heading photo by Taylor Hillier Photography

This book is dedicated to a dream that became a reality.

THIS BOOK CONTAINS:

Violence, alcohol abuse, death of a parent, dismemberment, genital mutilation, knife violence, mafia, murder, organized crime, sex work, verbal abuse, MMA fighting, group sex, touches on sex trafficking.

"Enough Alexey, I need him conscious and aware before he dies"- Anya Gorbachev

CHAPTER 1

ANYA

I have never believed in fate. Fate is for fools who believe in love at first sight, fools who believe that because monsters don't hide under the bed, they don't exist. I've always scoffed at such nonsense, even though the events leading up to my fall from grace could be considered just that.

I have had something of a grudge against destiny; ever since the fates were cruel enough to make me the sole; female heir to my father's empire. He had wanted a son and longed for a baby boy to pass his bloodstained crown to. Instead, he had me. Someday soon, I will be forced to marry a man of my father's choosing. Punishment for being a woman? Or just how things are done? It's not up to me to question these things. I suppose you could call that fate as well.

Nobody sees me as anything other than a woman who should know her place. I'm the daughter and only child of Anatoli Gorbachev, Pakhan of the Bratva, one of the most ruthless unyielding Mafia bosses to ever rule. This precarious position has given me many names. To him, I am Anya. His business associates, both the legitimate and the less savory, simply call me "Gorbachev's daughter." To them, I am just a pretty face. His princess. Little do they know that behind this pretty face, I am just like my father: fearless, cunning, ruthless, and unyielding. You will never see me coming.

To those who unfortunately cross my father, I go by another name altogether. If we meet in the dark of night, my face will be the last one you will ever see. I am Baba Yaga. I may not live in a hut with chicken legs, but I am far more dangerous. Baba Yaga can be a help or a hindrance, a curse or a boon. I imagine she is similar to what you Americans would call "the boogeyman." Only I am real. If you are sent to me, there is no second chance; it will be your execution.

In our circles, word travels on wings. Rumors and gossip fly especially fast. They say my father shed a tear when I was born. They say I am a cold bitch with no heart. Perhaps they are right. I keep people at a distance, and I have never lost sleep over the things I have done. I serve my father with unquestionable loyalty.

After strapping my kunai knives to my thigh, I run my fingers over the dresses in my closet. Most of them are red, tasteful corals to deep, lush crimson tones. Blood money

BABA YAGA

bought them, so it seems only fitting. Choosing a bloodred, knee-length dress, I slip it on and pair it with stiletto heels. Mask on. I need to prepare for my performance.

Today, my father has me smiling and schmoozing an up-and-coming fighter coming to Vegas for a shot at a title match. My father has several investments, and this faceless - and most likely obnoxious – fighter is his latest one. If it has the potential for profit, Anatoli's in on it, whether it's fighting, hotels, casinos, or prostitution. Most of Vegas's economy is connected to him, in one way or another.

As I grab my leather jacket, phone and keys, I can't seem to shake this gut feeling that I'm unprepared for what is next. In my line of work, I've come to trust my instincts. They're never wrong, and they've saved me more than once. As I step onto the elevator of my penthouse suite, I can't help thinking my life is about to change. I hope I am ready for it.

CHAPTER 2

LIAM

Fighting is in my blood. I knew the first time I got my ass handed to me standing up to a bully. I learned how to play the game and play it well when I was younger. Women may say I'm arrogant, cocky, and have an ego they can't compete with, but then again, they only see the version of me I want them to see. People love to hate me and judging by the sounds coming from the auditorium I just fought in, I'd say somebody lost a lot of money once again underestimating me. Ronan bursts into the room as I toss my hand wraps and shorts in my gym bag.

"It's turning into a mob out there, mate. We better make ourselves sparse. You've pissed off a few influential businessmen tonight by winning," he says laughing.

"Well, it's their bloody fault for betting against me ain't it" I quip back, slinging my bag over my shoulder as we make our way out back to my truck.

"Where's the old man?" looking around for my father.

"He was schmoozing some men in suits when I came back to get you. He can catch up, we need to go," he says hopping in the passenger seat.

The back doors crash open, and men file out with an ax to grind. There's my cue, so I throw the truck in gear and get us the fuck out of there.

We meet up with the rest of my team at Danvers Gym, giving high fives, and a round of shots to celebrate when my father, Declan, walks in preening like a peacock. He probably bet on me winning to get a payday.

"Well, son, you've finally done it," he says with a huge grin.

"Done what exactly?" I say, not in the mood for his word games tonight.

"Gotten the attention you've been looking for, boy. A representative of a very powerful man out in Vegas was watching you tonight. He liked what he saw, made a call, and I have secured you a fight in Las Vegas, which upon your victory, secures you a title shot. How does that sound, smartass?"

"It sounds fucking amazing if it's legit," I say, not quite believing what I'm hearing. Anything that sounds too good to be true usually is.

"You bet your ass. Hope all your passports are up to date because Vegas, here we come," he yells as he lifts a shot of whiskey to his lips.

Sarah Jane

I finally fucking did it. I salute my team with my shot, and we celebrate into the wee hours. Vegas won't know what hit them.

———

Four weeks later, the plane touches down in Las Vegas, and my adrenaline skyrocketed. This is my chance to prove myself. Nothing is more important to me than a shot at the title. They call me an up-and-coming fighter with the potential to be great. I hate to break it to these assholes, but I've been fighting my whole life. I come from nothing, and I sure as shit have more than just the potential to be great. I'm not being conceited. It's just a fact. I won't pussyfoot around anyone, and I've worked damn hard to get to where I am.

Fighting is all I've ever been good at. Don't get me wrong, I'm not a stupid guy, I just live for the fight. Preparing for it, walking in and hearing your name being shouted, sizing up your opponent, and the challenge to come out on top is my bread and butter. I'm in the best shape I've ever been in, and tonight will be the start of my rise to the top. I'm wound so tight I'm fit to burst.

My whole focus has been getting ready for this fight: clean eating, training hard, no alcohol, no drugs-not that I touch that shit anyway- and no pussy. That last one was the hardest. What can I say? I like fucking. When you're six feet, 175 lbs of muscle, and decorated in tattoos, the women eat that shit up.

After this fight, I am finding someone warm and willing to celebrate my victory before we head back to Ireland.

BABA YAGA

Declan O' Conner, my manager and father, has been in my ear the entire flight about not fucking this up. I'm more concerned about him placing bets and losing my money than I am about my fight tomorrow. He isn't a bad guy, just lost since my mum passed, even after all these years. He enjoys the drink a bit too much and loves gambling on anything from sports to pony races. I should fire him and get someone legit to represent me, but he's the only family I have, so I keep an eye on him and pick his ass up when he falls.

We walk off the plane, and I'm barely paying attention to the old man when he smacks me in the arm and yells "Have you heard a bloody word I've said?"

I give my head a quick shake and watch as his eyes almost roll completely back in his head. He hates when I don't listen to his bullshit, and I quite enjoy pissing him off. What else is family for?

He looks at me and says a very important man is sponsoring this fight, and I'm to show the appropriate respect, yadda yadda. I know what's riding on this fight, my whole future. I have done nothing but eat, sleep and breathe fighting in preparation for this. I will not let my nerves or my father get the best of me. I listen to him rattle on, and as I look up, I stop paying attention again. The sexiest woman I have ever seen is walking my way, flanked by two big-ass motherfuckers.

Pure Sin is how I would describe her. Close to my six feet with those stilettos she's wearing- yes, I know what the shoes are called, I pay attention- a bloodred dress that hugs every curve, leather jacket and if I'm not mistaken, ink peeking out the sleeves on both arms. Long dark hair, blue eyes, and full lips painted red like her dress. I stand a little straighter, and it has nothing to do with the two goliaths on either side of her.

CHAPTER 3

ANYA

My father insisted I bring his muscle with me like I cannot handle some MMA fighter. As if. I saved my breath though. Anatoli's word is the law.

We pull up to the loading zone at the airport, and Sergei throws the SUV in park. He gets out and comes around the front as Dmitry opens my door. As we approach the doors, they flank me on both sides, giving a clear message to anyone looking we are not to be fucked with.

The airport is packed as usual, scurrying around like mice in a cage. I'm annoyed already, thankfully, we are given a wide berth. I look up at the arrivals board, already dreading this bloody fiasco of a day. This errand is beneath me, and I'm frustrated and antsy. Locating the gate we need; I head in that direction. As I come upon the two men

I'm here to pick up, the younger of the two looks up. We make eye contact, and I feel a shift in my gut. I'm in deep shit.

I have a healthy sex drive, but I'm not one to swoon over any man. My extracurricular activity for my father makes it impossible for a relationship, so I'm a "get my oil changed and leave" kind of girl. But this man with piercing eyes, tattoos, and a wall of muscle is checking all my boxes.

His eyes roam my whole body from head to toe and back up. I know he likes what he sees. My body is a well-oiled machine, giving the illusion of feminine beauty, but deadly, nonetheless. I could snap your neck with my legs and not break a sweat.

His eyes get wide as we approach. He moves his left foot back just a little as he sizes up the two men on either side of me. Southpaw I, see? I find it hilarious that he's not aware I'm the dangerous one in the group.

His father, I'm assuming, turns and raises his hand to me, "Good afternoon, you must be our welcoming party. I'm Declan O'Conner, and this is my son, Liam. It's a pleasure to meet you."

I paste on my brightest smile and shake his hand. "Hello Mr. O'Conner. Welcome to Vegas. My name is Anya Gorbachev, Anatoli's daughter. I'm here to collect you both, show you around, and make sure you see all Vegas has to offer while you're here." I pause and then turn toward Liam and shake his hand as well.

He gives me another once over with his eyes. "It's nice to meet you".

I quickly go over his schedule on my phone making

sure nothing is left out. Once the pleasantries are over, we collect their bags and head to the car. Our SUV is outfitted like a limo, Liam, Declan and I climb in the back with me facing Liam and Dmitry gets in the front with Sergei. The first stop is checking into my father's hotel. I make idle chit-chat along the way and pretend I know nothing about UFC fighting to preserve the illusion of being just a pretty face. Liam tries to make eye contact as he speaks, but I avoid it. I feel as if he sees things I would rather keep hidden. I sense he's not buying the load of shit I'm shoveling him.

He has questions, that much I know, but thankfully we arrive, and the valet comes to open my door.

"Welcome back, Miss Gorbachev. Right this way, everything is prepared as you wished."

I thank him as Sergei and Dmitry come around to my sides again.

Welcome to Nopok, or in English, Vice: a man's ultimate candy land. My father spared no expense in building his empire here, choosing sleek black walls, emerald green furniture, gold accents, and crystal chandeliers that exude classic elegance and money. The hotel and convention center boasts every vice a man can want, from gambling halls, fights, restaurants, bars, and lounges. We have shows to take the mistress to, spas for the wife when you're stuck with her, shopping, access to girls, and strippers and everything is discrete as long rules are followed.

As we walk through the lobby past the waterfall that looks like it's dripping diamonds, I wonder what Liam thinks as his eyes take everything in. It shouldn't matter to me. He's only a distraction for a few days, but I am very curious indeed.

My mind is still wandering as Dmitry and Sergei escort us to the elevator. Once inside, they take their places at the door and key in the code leading up to the penthouses. Without even looking at Liam, I can feel the weight of his stare on me. It's almost like a physical caress. I don't like being in this cooped-up space with Liam and his father, but I try not to let it show and take a calming breath as the door opens to the top floor. They don't need to know the other suite up here belongs to me and that my father strategically put him here for me to keep a close eye on his investment.

"Dermo!" (shit) My senses are on overdrive. Liam oozes power, yet that elevator ride made me feel like the most powerful woman in the world. His eyes worshipped me. I could feel him over every inch of my body without him even lifting a finger, and I wanted him. I'm comfortable in my skin, yet I'm covered in goosebumps from this man. My body is a traitor, and my mind is having a full-fledged war weighing the options between feeding this need or locking it down now. From the second we locked eyes in the airport, I felt like he saw right through my façade as much as I can see through his.

Anatoli would not be pleased by this hiccup. I'm to do my job and nothing more. Why is it that the first time I'm tempted to dance with the devil and to hell with the consequences, it's with Liam O'Conner? The only truth here is hell is where we will both end up if my father ever caught wind I played with his new toy.

CHAPTER 4

LIAM

I think I'm in love. Well, maybe love is a strong word. I've never had such a visceral reaction to a woman before and counting the many reasons why this woman and situation is a bad idea would give me a headache. I need to adjust myself as soon as we get off this god-forsaken elevator. I'm overwhelmed by the smell of this woman; she reminds me of home; and smells like the meadow after the rain near where I live. I sound like a pussy just having these thoughts. I've been around many beautiful women but never felt out of control. I could picture it, turning into a bloody caveman, beating my chest, and throwing her over my shoulder to fuck her senseless. I wanted to expose every curve until she was wearing nothing but lipstick and those shoes. To spend hours exploring the raw need I have for her. My father being less than a foot away, only slightly deterred me. So, lost in my thoughts, I hadn't noticed the elevator had stopped, and I stood alone looking like a tool.

Anya stood in the hallway beside my father with her head tilted, looking at me. I could feel myself getting a little warm under the collar like I had been caught red handed, so I hurry off and hold my arm out.

"Ladies first," I say and follow her to one of two doors in the hallway. Anya uses a key card to open the door, opening it so we can follow her in.

Everything about this hotel is first class. After walking through the lobby and taking everything in, I'm feeling under-dressed and out-classed, a feeling I certainly don't like.

The first thing I notice is the floor-to-ceiling wall of windows overlooking the strip. This place is the shit. We get a short tour ending in a bedroom with a king-sized bed, which is where she finds me standing a few minutes later.

"Is there a problem with your room Mr. O'Conner?" she says in her husky voice with traces of her Russian accent.

"No, I mean, it's amazing. I'm just a little confused about the one bed and where my father is sleeping, 'cause he sure as fuck ain't sleeping with me," I say with a little chuckle. I look up to find her smirking at me like I'm simple, and it gets my back hairs up. I don't like it.

"Your father and your team have adjacent rooms one floor down; I will take him down momentarily. My cell number is on a business card by the phone should you have any questions."

I'm off-kilter and horny as fuck around this woman; she

BABA YAGA

needs to go before I do something stupid. The first thing is getting her out of the bedroom, so I walk past her and head to the mini fridge for a bottle of water that I have no plan of drinking.

She follows telling me that I'll be picked up for both my weigh-in tonight and then escorted to my fight tomorrow night, where her father Anatoli would like to have a word with me before I go into the ring and after the fight. For the time being, she'll be my "unofficial tour guide" for the rest of the evening.

I know what she can show me. Shit. Get your head out of the damn gutter, man. I nod and say thank you, watching her sinful hips sway as she moves to the door.

My father, who has been quiet for once, walks over to me and cuffs me upside the back of the head.

"Ouch, what the fuck was that for?" I tell him, and he rolls his eyes.

"I know that look, boy. Focus on your fight, not on her ass. I'm telling you right now, Liam," he orders as he points at her, "she is so fucking off-limits. I'm warning you, stay away."

I give him a nod, so he knows I heard him, but my mind is screaming *challenge fucking accepted.*

He grabs his bag, holds open the door for Anya, gives me one last hard look, and they both walk out the door. When I hear the door click, I walk over to the window and look down at the strip to get my head in the game.

No pussy is worth losing track of why I'm here and what I want. Maybe if I keep telling myself that, I'll finally believe it.

15

CHAPTER 5

ANYA

As we walk onto the elevator, O'Conner Senior turns to me debating whether he should acknowledge what just happened. He decides to confront me.

"I know you heard me, lass, and I mean no disrespect. But you are trouble, with a capital T. That kind of trouble will have me, and my boy was never seen again."

I mull that over for a second, look at him, and simply nod my head. I'm not insulted. He is not as stupid as he seems. To get involved with me and mine is not to be taken lightly.

I show him to his room and tell him I will be back shortly to escort them to the weigh-in.

I was to greet Liam at the airport, get him and his father back to the hotel, situated in their rooms, and make sure he gets to his weigh-in. It's a mix of babysitting and ass-kissing. With the first of my obligations taken care of for the moment, I make my way down to my office just off the security rooms.

Nodding to Sergei and Dmitry, at their usual posts, I make my way into my office, closing the door behind me. Two steps in, I realize I'm not alone. As I spin to meet my intruder, he grabs me by my throat. I'm pushed against the wall and lifted off my feet.

"Tut Tut tuts, my *Printsessa*. You are losing your edge, no?" My father's right-hand man, Vlad, says with his usual slimy smirk. He's not squeezing hard, allowing me to smile like the predator I am.

"Not fucking likely, Butcher." To drive my point home, I tap his femoral artery with the knife he didn't even see me draw.

He slowly releases and lowers me to my feet as he turns to take a seat in my chair like a king on his throne. Vlad is how I would describe evil incarnate. He makes me feel like a child when near him, at 6'3", 230 pounds of solid muscle, and eyes the color of coal. An incredibly attractive man but with no soul. He demands respect with fear, and besides my father, he's the only man I'm truly afraid of.

"What the fuck do u want, Vlad? I don't need to be checked up on," I say as I slide into another chair and tap my knife on my crossed leg. I don't know why I push him the way I do. I just refuse to show fear.

"One day, you will be mine, Anya, and I will have to do something about that smart mouth of yours. I will enjoy breaking you, princess." He stands, proceeds to do up his suit jacket, smiles at me, and walks out.

SARAH JANE

Once the door closes, I let the shudder his words give me to pass along my spine. That man creeps me out, and that's saying something. They don't call Vlad "the butcher" for nothing. He has been my father's right hand for as long as I can remember. Vlad is the wall between our enemies and my father. He is also the man my father has promised my hand to. My father says the man to take his place must be unwavering in his loyalty to the Bratva. He must be strong, command respect, and know his place by my side. My father is a fool. Vlad will stomp me into submission the day I'm handed over. I do not trust him. I am afraid of him. My days are numbered.

CHAPTER 6

LIAM

Most men would say yoga is for pussies, but they would be fucking wrong. With my tunes blaring I get in the right head space, shut out the noise, and stretch out to begin. Each pose is natural to me. I breathe in and out, going over my fight plan, loosening up my muscles, and releasing the stress. I'm so focused as I move into a downward dog position that, at first, I don't acknowledge the feeling I'm being watched, so when I take a look between my legs, I'm surprised to see Anya leaning against the bar with a look on her face I could get behind. I move to stand, stretching my arms over my head. If the lady is going to look, I'll make sure she gets a damn eye full.

"Enjoying the view, love?" I ask, strolling past her to the bedroom.

"Not likely, little man. I knocked nobody answered. I'm here to collect you for your weigh-in," she says, faking boredom.

I laugh at her, knowing full well this woman is anything but bloody bored.

"I'll take a quick shower and be good to go." I drop my boxer briefs with a quick look over my shoulder to make sure her eyes are where they should be.

"For the record, there's nothing little about it, princess," I say and walk away.

A quick very cold shower later, and I'm dressed, meeting her by the door. I follow her into the elevator, wait for the doors to close, and turn to say something but stop in my tracks when I see the look on her face. I don't know what happened between flirting, the shower, and now, but her eyebrows are drawn together, and scowling. She looks pissed.

We ride in silence down to the lobby, where we meet up with Senior and the two gorillas following Anya around, and head to the conference room.

As we take our seats on the stage, my eyes follow Anya to where she sits beside two men. One I'm assuming is my sponsor, her father, and the other is one ugly mean-looking motherfucker who makes a point to bare his fucking teeth at me when he catches where I'm looking.

So, the princess has a fan. Almost makes this way more fun. I smirk at him and turn to see my opponent come up on stage with his coach.

Pleasantries are exchanged, and we both make weight, naturally. We stand facing each other, fists up for the photo op. A few questions are asked by the press, some smack

BABA YAGA

talk for the fans, and we're done till fight time. I'm jacked on adrenaline, and all pumped up now for this fight. Nothing is going to bring me down.

That is until I see Anya and what looks like a brick wall army heading straight for me.

———

ANYA

Heading into the auditorium for weigh-in has me all out of sorts. No man should have the right to look so damn sexy while doing yoga, and that ass, good lord. All I could do was stare and take in all the hard lean muscle and the tattoos. Don't get me started on the tattoos he's covered. He's a work of art. Shit, I need to focus.

Declan doesn't know how accurate he was. My thoughts would have me in deep water and Liam's head on a platter. Vlad sees me as property; he'd fuck him up on principle alone, and blatantly ignoring my father's orders is not an option, so I give my head a mental shake and paste a smile on my face as I walk over to my father. We grasp elbows, and I lean in to kiss him on his cheek.

"Hello, Father. How are you today?"

Anatoli is a big man, not just in height and bulk. He's larger than life, untouchable almost, but at the end of the day he's just Father to me, and I am his everything.

"You get more beautiful every day, daughter. So much like your mother," he responds in his usual manner.

SARAH JANE

I never knew my mother. She died when I was very young, but I've heard this every day of my life.

He ushers me to a chair where we all sit to watch his investment do his weigh-in. My father speaks to Vlad, whom I have yet to acknowledge, about both fighters- their strengths, weaknesses, and high hopes for a good fight. My head spins when I hear a growl come from Vlad, and my father's robust laugh follows. I follow their line of sight and see Liam smirking at Vlad before he turns to meet my eyes.

"Jealousy is ugly on you, Vlad," my father says as I catch up on what just happened.

"That would insinuate I feel threatened by the little man, boss. I merely don't like his eyes on what's mine," Vlad calmly and coolly responds.

"And that would insinuate Vlad, that I'm yours to be concerned over, to begin with," I respond in the sweetest and most mocking tone I can muster.

My father looks amused by our little banter but directs us back to the matter at hand. We stand as the interview portion ends and proceed toward Liam and his father for a little chat. Vlad attempts to place his hand on my lower back and lead me. Luckily, I'm quite graceful and sidestep to get up beside my father, leaving him in the back with Dmitry and Sergei. I see Declan turn to Liam and say something I can't quite hear. Liam stands a little taller. I can imagine seeing my father and his brick wall army coming your way would make anyone stand a little taller. He should be afraid. Only a dead man would not falter in the face of Anatoli Gorbachev. Declan moves to intercept us, holding out his hand for my father to shake.

Baba Yaga

"Good afternoon, Mr. Gorbachev. So nice to finally meet in person and thank you for all your support."

My father hates nothing more than a kiss ass, but he did give his support. Much to my surprise, he raises his hand for a handshake.

"No need to thank me, Declan I hear great things about your boy. I'm looking forward to the fight. If you'd do the introductions, I'd like to meet him."

Sensing, he's being dismissed, Declan slowly walks toward Liam.

"Liam, this is Mr. Gorbachev, your sponsor for this fight and the man footing the bill for your big break."

I'm intrigued by how Liam will handle that gentle jab his father just gave him but also impressed with the power he exudes, especially up against one of the most ruthless leaders in Mafia history.

Liam

"Holy mother fucking shit. Keep calm, keep calm," I silently tell myself.

This man will eat me for breakfast and give the leftovers to the giants flanking him if I show any fear. Time to put up or shut up, stand tall and handle my shit.

I raise my hand to shake his. "It's a pleasure to meet you, sir." Yes, I have manners. "Thank you for the opportunity and support you've given."

With a firm handshake, he looks me over and says, "I quite look forward to watching you fight, boy. I hear great things about you."

I maintain eye contact, waiting for him to say more, but he's interrupted by the growly one trying to put his mitts on Anya. They whisper a few words, and Anatoli turns to me.

"I have urgent business to attend to, so you'll have to excuse me. Anya, you will come with me now. She will be back to collect you shortly."

I am effectively dismissed, but I don't miss the look my way from Anya or the grizzly bear as they all walk away.

I remain calm and impartial till they are out of hearing range and then turn to my father and say, "What the fuck have you gotten me into, Da?"

"I don't know what you're on about, Liam, but u best be showing me some respect. I got you this gig," he says.

I know something isn't right here.

"You've done something. Those are not the type of men you get involved with. You fuck up, and you're never heard from again. What the fuck were you thinking?"

I'm wound up now, but every instinct I have is screaming this is a bad idea, and this all hinges on me winning this fight. I walk away from my father, but I don't get too far before I feel him step in place beside me. I head to the elevators, push the button, and get my head in the game. I have a fight to win.

CHAPTER 7

ANYA

As we leave the auditorium, people stare and very quickly move out of our way as we head down the main lobby corridor. No matter how old I get, it still amazes me how much power my father exudes simply by being. He still hasn't told me why I'm needed, but as we turn toward his office, I have a feeling somebody is about to have a bad night.

Sergei and Dmitry open the double doors and take up their stations on each side. Anatoli walks to his polished gold bar cart and pours a shot of billionaire vodka. My father had humble beginnings, but looking at him now, taking a shot of vodka worth millions, he's dripping in wealth and only has the best of everything. After two shots, he sets his shot glass down, navigates around his monstrosity of a desk, and sits on his "throne." I take a seat on the other side, turning to Vlad as he takes the other seat.

"I didn't know this matter needed to include you, Vlad. You may go," I say, thus, dismissing him.

Never allowing me the last word, I can almost feel him smirking before he says, "Ah, *Printsessa*, you forget I don't work for you, and do keep in mind, I will be in charge one day. Don't continue to push me."

"Fuck. Enough, both of you. Vlad, you remember your place. I am not dead yet, so you control nothing." Father slams his hands on the table before turning to me.

"Anya, you would be wise not to antagonize Vlad." He shakes his head as if wanting to say more but simply says, "Now, back to the matter at hand."

"Alexey has informed me that a regular customer of Sasha, Mr. Kolinski, has beaten her bloody, leaving her unconscious before attempting to flee. He has been warned before. We have rules for a reason, and to disrespect me in such a fashion demands a response." my father says with such venom in his voice I almost feel sorry for the idiot.

Alexey is one of my father's captains who oversees running the girls. We are Russian, so of course, we run girls, but our girls are not only clean, smart, and sexy, they also walk into this wide open, so to speak, and are compensated well for it.

Fucking coward, hitting a woman because your dick doesn't work the way it should. I don't have to look up to know my father is not only disgusted but severely angry. Our best money maker now needs a surgery consult in plastics.

BABA YAGA

"Death". One word from my father, and I know Mr. Kolinski is about to meet my other side.

"Da, it will be done."

I stand up, smooth out my dress, and walk towards the door. I look back for a second to see both men staring after me, one with a look of pride and the other like I'm his last meal.

I nod at the guards on watch and proceed to security to see if Alexey has returned with my prey for the evening. As it turns out, Alexey was not only successful in grabbing our wayward man but he's all comfortable waiting for me.

I walk to my office, shutting myself in before crossing to the back wall behind my desk. Pushing on a section and entering my pin reveals a door and passageway to my fun room.

The *"Komnata Smerti" (Room of death)* is a large round room underneath the hotel with access from the private offices and a secret way in through the delivery area. I have a table along one side with my favorite knives and instruments to use.

The crime determines how long I make someone suffer. On the far wall, I have a roulette wheel for extraction of information games, along with some shock "therapy" tools. A chair sits smack dab in the middle over the drain where all the blood runs. It never gets old to me, that utter look of confusion as they sit there waiting for the death they know is coming from "Baba Yaga," and then I walk in looking the way I do. It's almost laughable when they smile and thinks they are dodging a bullet. After all, it's only Anatoli's "princess". I let them savor it for a moment or two.

Today is no different. I walk into the room to find Alexey with his sleeves rolled up and knuckles all bloody after having a minor discussion with Mr. Kolinski's very swollen face.

"Enough, Alexey, I need him conscious and aware before he dies."

"Of course, I was just paying in kind for the mess he left on Sasha's face." He straightens and smiles at me over his shoulder.

Alexey is a beautiful man if men can be called such things, but alas, he is a mouse-controlled by lions.

By this time, Mr. Kolinski has managed to raise his head and sees me standing there.

"Anya, I mean Miss Gorbachev, thank goodness you are here. Please tell your father this is all a simple misunderstanding. I pay girls well, so why am I being so mistreated over a prostitute?"

"Mr. Kolinski, I see you are confused, about why I am here." I pause long enough to unzip my dress, hang it on the peg, and put my uniform, so to speak, on. "I am not here for negotiations nor the ramblings of a coward."

"Then why would Anatoli send a woman, ugh."

I hear blood being spat on the floor.

"Don't interrupt the lady, Kolinski" Alexey says, amused.

I saunter over to my table of tools, feeling Kolinski's eyes following me the whole time, and absently tap my kunai knife on my chin, drawing out my decision. This piece of shit deserves my best performance yet. Sasha isn't just our best most requested girl, she is also my friend, and right now, her beautiful face is unrecognizable.

BABA YAGA

My eyes roam over the table twice and land on a very fitting tool. I look over my shoulder at Kolinski and give him my best smile, and his face drains of color. I put my knife back in the holster strapped to my thigh and pick up the Burdizzo on my right.

As I turn, Alexey sees what's in my hand and proceeds to laugh. "Ah Baba Yaga, you never cease to amaze me. May I stay and watch the show?"

"Wait, wait, wait. You're Baba Yaga? That can't be right. No bitch is worth my death," Kolinski screeches as he finally catches up to what is happening and starts to struggle in the chair.

"Now, Kolinski, I'm slightly offended you're not taking this seriously. That bitch is my friend, and you know what happens when you break the rules and cross Anatoli." I start walking toward him, slowing while swinging the Burdizzo. "Men like you think you are better, superior. Well, I'm about to show you what a real bitch is." I have Alexey remove the panel on the underside of the chair, so I have access to his disgusting shriveled-up dick. "Burdizzo's, Kolinski, are used in castrating livestock, and I feel it fitting that you should die from the sorry excuse of a dick that got you in this mess. Scream. Nobody can hear you."

Alexey tilts the chair back, and I clamp the Burdizzo around his testicles snipping them right off. Blood runs all over the floor, and Kolinski is howling, begging, crying, and bleeding out.

Not feeling like my point has been made, I say, "Alexey, tip that chair back again."

I pull my kunai knife out and slice off his manhood as well, then place it in his lap.

SARAH JANE

I look over, and Alexey looks a little green. He backs up and washes off his hands in the sink. I pull a chair over and sit and watch as Kolinski stares at his cock, bleeding out. I'm a monster, I know, but what I did was no less than he deserved.

"Dasvindaniya."

Once he takes his last breath, Alexey calls in the clean-up crew, and I grab my dress, needing a shower.

"Anya," Alexey calls to me.

"Yes, Alexey?" I look at him.

After a breath, he says, "I've seen some fucked up shit, but that was crazy. How do you sleep at night?"

"Who says I do, Alexey? I do what needs to be done. I'm Bratva, no mercy. Just hope you never have to see me come in this door for you," I say and leave the room.

———

I shower using the bathroom in my office to wash off the stink and black thoughts clouding my mind. After I dry off, I take a long look in the mirror to apply my makeup and do my hair.

With my mask firmly back in place, I head to my father's office to let him know it has been done. I approach his office and raise my fist to knock but pause when I hear my father talking to someone telling them to make sure Liam's father gets in deep, with no limit, and make damn sure he ends up indebted to him and the Bratva.

A shiver goes straight down my spine. Why does my father want that man to owe him? Then I realize it's Liam he's after, and lord fucking help him if my father gets that wish.

I knock and wait for his command to enter. After hearing "enter," I stroll in as he hangs up his phone.

"Is it done?" he says calmly, leaning back in his chair.

"Yes, Father. Clean-up is being handled as we speak. May I?" I point to his bar. He nods, and I walk over to pour myself a shot and bring him one as well.

"Very good, Anya. Now tonight, I need you to take the fighter to dinner and make sure he's back to his room early. Big night tomorrow."

"And Mr. O' Conner?" I say while watching my father's face for any idea of what he has planned.

"The father is to be shown all the perks of being a guest at Vice."

Just what I thought I had heard. Without giving away what I had overheard, I nod to my father, thank him for the drink, and prepare to leave.

"I see your mind working Anya. You are my child, leave it be and do as you've been told." Dismissing me, he turns to the window and absently stares outside.

I make my way back down the hall and stop at security to get an all-clear. Then I walk past the front desk, making sure everyone is good. With nothing to report, I head for the elevators.

CHAPTER 8

LIAM

I'm on edge. Everything about this deal- sponsorship, whatever you want to call it seems dodgy as fuck. I have questions and no answers. My father has his lips sealed tighter than a nun's legs, which only raises more questions. I don't doubt my skill or getting to this point, but the secrecy surrounding the deal and my father's evasiveness have my instincts on overdrive. My father has outdone himself this time. I dropped him off at his room after the weigh-in, pissed off with the no-fucks-given attitude he has right now.

I'm stewing over everything, looking out the window at the lights below, when there's a knock at the door. I open it to find Anya wearing a floor-length red dress, her hair

BABA YAGA

falling in waves, and not a thing out of place. She looks almost cold, so I try to lighten the mood.

I lean my head out the door and, in an out-of-character voice, say, "Excuse me, miss, but I believe you have the wrong room. Are you lost?"

There's a slight twitch in her mouth. She wants to smile at me because I'm acting like a tit. It's there and then gone.

"I'm here to grab you and take you to dinner," she says, sounding bored.

I allow her in and tell her I'll quickly change, so we can go. She nods and walks over to look out the windows.

Once I change and return to the room, she's standing in the same place I left her. "Shall we go?"

Anya nods, and we make our way out the door to the elevator.

I've never had trouble with women. Reading their body language was something I could brag about. These few glimpses past the mask Anya wears make me feel like a junkie, waiting for his next fix. It's ridiculous, but I want to push. I want to see that smile she tries so hard to hide. I want, I want, I want.

We ride the elevator down to the lobby in silence. When we step off, I gently place my hand on her lower back. For a split second, she stiffens but allows it. We walk down a long hallway off to the right of the lobby. Each side seems to branch out to lounges, restaurants, and a spa. A sign directs where my fight will be tomorrow night, but we take a left and arrive at an Italian restaurant called Luciano's. I find it odd Russians would have an Italian restaurant, but Anya's father has everything here. The maître d' greets us, and we follow along.

33

SARAH JANE

I hear my father's voice before I see him, and by the higher-than-normal octave, he's already in his cups. Fucking awesome. I pull out the chair for Anya. As she slides in, I give my father what I hope is the look of death should he decide to act like a nob.

"Liam, Anya, so glad you could join me. Now I don't have to eat alone," he says and lifts his glass to signal the waiter that he'd like another.

I order water, and Anya orders a vodka soda. I quickly scan the menu, hoping that if we eat quickly, I can get Anya out of here and my father to bed before he really gets going. Orders are placed, and before I can open my mouth to guide the conversation, Anya pipes up and asks my father about our life in Ireland and how I came to be a fighter.

I sip my water as I listen to Da tell her of our home.

"Not much to say about Ireland. Anything I loved about it died when my Grace took her last breath." He takes a slow sip of his drink before he continues, "She was the light in my world. I knew from the first moment she was mine and I was hers. Although it took a little convincing on my part." He chuckles.

"We knew everything as young people tend to think, and when Liam came kicking and screaming into this world, we foolishly thought nothing would ever separate us."

My memories of her are fading, but when he speaks of her like this, I can almost picture her. Anya is enamored and peppering him with questions, which gives me this overwhelming sense of gratitude. He needs to talk about her like this more often.

BABA YAGA

"I lost my mother when I was young as well. It leaves a hole that can't be filled. I'm so sorry for your loss, Declan," Anya says with a sadness we all share before changing the subject.

"I imagine raising this one had its challenges. How did Liam learn to fight, and what do you think about it?" She nods toward me before shooting my father a wink.

Setting his napkin down, he laughs wholeheartedly. "He was a small wiry ball of energy with one too many visits to the headmaster's office until I got a call one day saying Liam had been in a fight. I trucked my ass down to the school, ready to give him another whooping when I found him and a much smaller kid sitting there with bags of peas on their eyes and a much bigger lad smirking. It was clear what had happened, and my boy has been scrapping ever since.

Everyone underestimates my son. He's always seen as the underdog, which is their number one mistake. As for how I feel about it, I'm proud of my son. I just wish Grace were here to see the man he has become" His voice trails off in silent memory.

That fight changed the course of my life. I started going down to the local gym, shadowed the fighters, pissed off more than my fair share of people, and eventually, a man by the name of Danvers laid down the law. The rest is history. I went every day, soaking up the knowledge and learning every fighting style available to me. I was never that weak kid ever again. I'm so lost in my musings that I miss what my father just told Anya. What I didn't miss, though, was the genuine smile and the sound of her laughter.

35

SARAH JANE

One of two things happened after. First, I want to hear that sound again. Second, the look of pure shock on her face and those at the tables around us. Her mask had fallen, and holy fuck.

Food arrives, and we eat in comfortable silence. I ordered a mountain of pasta with chicken and vegetables. It's delicious, and the company ain't bad either.

———

ANYA

I don't remember the last time I laughed and judging by the looks on some of my father's business associates and regular guests nearby, neither do they. I look over at Liam, and after a brief look of shock, he returns my smile. In that moment, I can see the scrappy fighter with a will stronger than most grown men, and it's beautiful. I'm sure many women have fallen for this man with a smile like that alone. He reads me too well if he can see beyond the resting bitch face I've perfected over the years. I let people see what I want them to see.

My mind wanders as I take in the people around us. So many sheep and my father, the shepherd. I doubt they realize when coming to Vegas just how dangerous it can be. One wrong bet, one slip in the bed with a hooker, playing in the wrong playground, and you're owned or dead.

I give my attention back to Declan, who is on his way to sloppy drunk, muttering to himself. I lean over slightly to

BABA YAGA

make out what he's saying, and I hear him chastising himself over his fuck ups and the messes his son must clean up. He did one thing right, he mumbles, he raised a much better man than he is.

I'm learning so much from these men that were strangers just hours ago. My childhood was structured and almost military. Perfection was expected. I could throw a knife and shoot a gun with great accuracy by the age of nine. I graduated early and could best most men in hand-to-hand combat. This reprieve and chance to look through a window into someone else's life is unsettling but informative. As Declan begins to launch into another story Liam leans over.

"Da, we should get you to bed big day tomorrow."

And I thawed a little more until I lifted my eyes to see Vlad strutting his way toward the table. He pastes on a smile, which he thinks is charming but looks fake and painful to anyone looking at it.

"What do you want, Vlad?"

"That's no way to greet me, Anya. Do better next time. I'm here to collect Declan and give him the grand tour of what Vise has to offer," he says with just enough bite and bittersweetness.

My father has somebody watching me, and I don't fucking like it one bit. I know my job and my place. I look over to Liam, who looks like he's about to protest this new development. As our eyes meet, I give a subtle shake of my head and look up at Vlad.

"Of course, what a very good lap dog you are, Vlad."

I don't miss the chuckle from Liam or the growl from Vlad as I stand.

SARAH JANE

"I'm bored of this conversation. Goodnight, Declan. It's been a pleasure. Liam, this way, please, big day tomorrow."

I turn and walk away, ending any chance for a remark from Vlad. I can feel Liam step in place beside me as we make our way back to the elevators.

We make it to the elevators in strained silence. I can't help noticing our reflection in the elevator doors. He's in black slacks that fit perfectly, and a gray button-down dress shirt rolled up at the sleeves, highlighting strong and tattooed forearms. As he stands behind me and to the side, I can't help but muse over the fact we look good side by side. Powerful even.

When the elevator arrives, we step in. As the doors close Liam turns to me.

"I don't like being handled, Anya. What just happened, and why do I get the feeling I'm not going to like it," he says.

He's tense and slightly angry. I don't blame him; he sees more than he should. My father won't like this.

He's not wrong. However, I can't tell him the truth, and I'm not a liar either, so I settle for a half-truth.

"My father takes special interest in all avenues of his business. He wants Declan happy so you're happy, and it's a win for him. My advice is don't bite the hand that feeds you."

This doesn't appease him. He's tense, taking deep breaths, and won't make eye contact. Any joy from earlier has been sucked from the space. I can't allow myself to give a shit, so I drop him at his door.

"Goodnight, Liam. Tomorrow, we see if you're worth the effort." With that, I leave.

Chapter 9

Liam

I didn't sleep a wink last night. This whole fiasco has me on edge. I don't know what state my father is in this morning or, what mess I'm going to have to clean up. I'm tense and pissed off. Something about that growly asshole and Anya rubs me the wrong way, and the complete shutdown after he graced us with his fucking presence pisses me off further. I need to give my head a shake and remember why I'm here. It's fight night, so I'll get my ass up, not sleeping anyway, and get to it.

I start with stretches and yoga to get my blood flowing and loosen the muscles. They have a training facility here, so I'll make my way down there. I'll punch a few things and see if my training team has arrived and if they're ready to warm up with me. They came on a later flight than us and should have arrived late last night.

After a few wrong turns and some frustration, I finally find the training center and it doesn't disappoint. It's like my own personal Candyland. I do a full lap to get my bearings, trying to be respectful of the two people sparring in the cage. My team still hasn't arrived, so I pop in my earbuds and get to work. Fight days are usually light, but I do need to move my body, focus my brain, and loosen all my muscles. The training program I've done in preparation for this fight has been intense. Nothing, but my best performance is acceptable tonight. I run through some stretches, a round on each bag, and walk over to pick up the rope. With my music playing, I'm in the zone until my eyes wander over, finally getting a good look at who is sparring in the cage, and I'm jarred to a halt.

Beautiful is the only word I can use to explain what I'm seeing, and I sound like such a pussy for even thinking it, but it just is. Her jabs are smooth, and her movements so fluid between each transition. It's hard not to stare. I've never met a woman that had any real interest in fighting besides being arm candy for a fighter. And here is the woman, invading way too many of my thoughts lately sparring with a man twice her size and looking fucking graceful while doing it.

Well, now my dick is hard. I need to leave and get my head out of the gutter. I'm almost to the door when I hear Anya yell something in Russian. I turn around to see the big ugly fucker snickering at her beside the cage. The guy training with her then makes the mistake of snickering too, and Anya turns to him, climbs up his front, wraps her legs around his neck, and flips herself backward, taking him flying over the front of her. It looks like a scene from an action movie. Looking back now this should have been my first sign she was more than she appeared. He hits the mat hard, and since I'm immature as shit sometimes, I proceed to clap and laugh my arse off.

Anya looks up, almost happy with my response, before quickly schooling her features. The ugly fucker- I know his name, but I ain't saying it, so ugly fucker works- is now turned toward me, giving me a look that I imagine would make most men piss their pants, but I've never let anyone intimidate me. I'm not starting now either.

"I don't think the lady appreciated being laughed at," I say as I lean against the door frame to the exit. "Or whatever u said beforehand."

"эти чертовы дни сочтены, и он даже не знает об этом" *this fucker's days are numbered, and he doesn't even know it* he says to the group of men with him. "Mind your business, little man." in a mocking tone.

Even though I know that's not what he just said, I don't have to say anything because he turns back to bickering in Russian with Anja. I make my exit while I can and head to my room for a late breakfast.

CHAPTER 10

ANYA

The incident at the gym has me feeling out of sorts. Russian men would never encourage a woman to do what I just did. They certainly wouldn't clap and laugh. Liam looked almost proud, clearly amused. It's not something I'm accustomed to. Vlad was decidedly not amused and was sure to let me know.

I leave the gym and am almost to the elevator when my cell alerts me with a text.

Father:

Downstairs now

BABA YAGA

Looks like somebody's day just got worse.

I think Alexey was disappointed with my lack of flare this time around. I didn't ask what the man had done or why his boss was there being held at gunpoint to drive home whatever point my father was trying to make. I simply walked in, picked up my gun, shot the man in the head, and walked out. I'm sure I'll hear from my father when I arrive at the fight tonight, but I can't muster the energy to give a fuck right now.

Something has shifted in me; in the span of forty-eight hours, I've laughed and felt more freedom than I've ever known. It scares me to notice just how hollow and black my soul has become. I don't want to admit the cause, nor do I want to address it right now.

I've just finished curling my hair and pinning it as an ode to the '50s pin-up, and I walk over to my closet to select a dress I know will cause a reaction. It's emerald green, halter-style, with an opening clear to my navel, open back, and slits straight up to my hip. Not my usual red color, but I'm feeling lucky, so I nabbed this dress from our in-house boutique. I never go anywhere without my knives, so I attach what will look like a garter to anyone looking but holds my kunai perfectly and within reach. A swipe of blood-red lipstick and sky-high stilettos, and I'm ready. I make my way down to the lobby, step off the elevator, and immediately Sergei and Dmitry take their places on either side of me. I don't miss their intake of breath from Dmitry or how Sergei averts his eyes. I also don't miss the looks of appreciation from every man we pass or looks of envy from

SARAH JANE

women either. ick glance in a mirror as I walk by, and my breath catches. I know I'm beautiful, and, in this moment I'm powerful. I'm fashionably late, as is a woman's prerogative. As I enter the arena, the cheering, screaming, and sounds of pounded flesh envelop me. I walk towards my father and Vlad in our front-row seats, and the moment Vlad sees me, I smirk. He's pissed, nostrils flaring as he takes in my dress, and I can't help the pure joy pissing him off gives me. I hold onto that feeling.

"What the fuck do you think you are doing dressing like a common whore?" Vlad says as he grabs my arm.

"So good to see you, as usual, Butcher, but must I remind you yet again, I'm owned by no man and won't be told how to dress. Besides, I look good. Every man here knows it."

"Remove your hand from my daughter, Vlad, before I break it," my father says as he approaches me. "You look more and more like your mother, my beautiful daughter." He offers me his hand and helps me to my seat at his side.

"I understand the lateness of your arrival. Alexey reported our problem was handled however underwhelming. I trust there was a reason for your lack of enthusiasm in this matter."

He's so casual as he says it, but I know my father wants an answer, and it better please him.

"Not every situation requires theatrics, Father. The man Sergei held up by his shirt collar was scared he was next. He pissed his pants when I shot his associate, so I think your point was sufficiently made," I say calmly.

He simply nods and turns back in time to listen to the results of the last fight.

BABA YAGA

We all stand and clap as the crowd goes wild, and my father receives the cursory head nod and acknowledgment of respect from the fighters and their teams as they leave the octagon. As I said, everyone owes my father something.

We wait as the order is restored in preparation for the next fight. The lights dim, and Ed Sheeran's "Galway Girl" comes over the speakers. I can't help the smile that forms on my face. Of course, this is his song. I crane my head so I can get a good look at Liam as he makes his way to the octagon.

He's flanked by four men, all with athletic builds, and strolling down the walkway toward the cage. No arrogance or sign of the cocky man most think him to be. He looks calm but pulsing with energy. Declan follows at a slight distance, not exactly being subtle with the slight meandering. Just before Liam gets to the cut man, Declan catches up and says something to Liam. It's too loud in here to hear, but it's clear Liam either doesn't hear him or doesn't give a fuck. Their relationship both confuses and fascinates me. Such blunt honesty and disrespect would never be tolerated in my world. But the passion they both show in life, good or in Declan's case very bad is to be envied. The only passion I have is the brutality I show my father's enemies.

I'm lost in both thought and watching Liam take his shirt off, as the cut man applies Vaseline and inspects his gloves, so I don't realize Declan has wandered over and taken the vacant seat beside me.

"I wonder how many of these tossers bet money my son is losing this fight?" He smiles mockingly, looking around before taking a hefty swig of his whiskey.

"Some advice for you, Declan, watch your mouth here. You are not in Ireland anymore and lay off the booze. Do try to be professional," I say nonchalantly and loud enough for only us to hear.

He gives me a nod, which I figure will be the best I'm going to get, so we both turn back to the fight. The introductions have begun, and Liam is bouncing back and forth, warming up as they call Ivan's name and his stats. They meet in the middle, touch gloves, and move into position. The fight is five rounds at five minutes starting with the usual dance around each other, watching foot placement, and a couple of swings testing each other out. Ivan looks over, giving a subtle nod to my father, which causes Liam to look over. Those two seconds give Ivan the opening he needs, landing a right hook to Liam's chin.

Declan is on his feet. "Get your head in the game, Liam, for fuck's sake!"

Liam looks dazed for a second or two, and then a rage I'm all too familiar with comes over his features. Pushing forward, he lands a combo to Ivan's chin, ribs, and head while Ivan tries to pivot and miscalculates.

His team is making calls to Liam, but I can't hear them over the commentary from Declan beside me.

Ivan retaliates, landing a few jabs to Liam's side, and attempts a takedown which Liam anticipates. With a quick sidestep, he throws a left hook to Ivan's jaw and a hard kick to his right side.

Ten seconds to go in the first round, and it's back and forth. Ivan is bleeding from a shot to the temple, and Liam has an injury to his right eye. The horn sounds and both fighters head to their corners for water. The cut man evalu-

BABA YAGA

ates Ivan's cut and talks to him. I imagine he's coaching him on what to do in the next round.

"It seems your son's reputation is well-founded," I say to Declan without taking my eyes off the cage.

"Liam should never be underestimated. He will always prove you wrong," he responds with conviction.

Liam's head turns and our eyes lock. I nod my head, and he returns it. The horn sounds again, signaling the start of round two.

That first round was fast-paced, even my father looks impressed. Liam is proving to be well worth the effort now. Whether this works out well for him or not remains to be seen.

I'm fidgeting in my seat, I want to cheer for him and shit-talk the other fighter. But I have no idea what possessed me to want to do these things. I mean, I shot a guy in the head this afternoon and went for a pedicure after. So many things are out of character for me lately.

Liam stands up, moving back into his fighting position, with Ivan following suit. I inspect Liam once again, pausing to finally admire the ink covering his body. He has a fierce lion mid-roar, covering his whole back, with a crown on its head. King of the jungle he definitely is. There are Celtic symbols, ropes intertwined, his mother's name - Grace- on his arm, and his chest, he has Puck O' Conner with leaves, shamrocks, and things I can't quite make out from here. Won't stop me from imagining, though, what it would feel like to lick him from navel to throat.

Ivan comes out swinging, obviously disappointed with how the first round ended. He lands a few jabs and a leg kick to Liam's right leg, but Liam just smirks and settles into a good back-and-forth with Ivan. Jabs and leg kicks go back and forth, Liam sweeps his leg, taking Ivan to the ground, and they grabble around before getting back on their feet.

Vlad is cursing in Russian. He's not happy the fighter he backed hasn't taken this fight yet. He doesn't take looking like a fool well. If Ivan loses, I'd hate to be him. The butcher is someone even I'm afraid of.

I keep taking side glances at my father, trying to judge his mood and thoughts on the fight, but he's locked down all emotion and seems to be looking at the fight rather clinically. He looks over his shoulder at Sergei gives a slight head nod and turns back to see me.

"Enjoying the fight daughter?" he says with his head slightly tilted. I can't show too much enthusiasm or interest, so I respond with veiled sarcasm.

"It's entertaining, and the people are getting their money's worth. They are well matched, but we both know they are no match for me."

He chuckles and pats my hand "How very true that is, my Anya."

Returning our attention to the fight, I'm doing my best to ignore the vile comments Vlad's hurling at Ivan. Both fighters are here because of my father, regardless of Vlad's thoughts on the matter. It's business and numbers to him.

The second-round finishes and both men are sweaty. The wink I get from Liam sets Vlad off on another tirade, but my father is amused, so I say nothing.

BABA YAGA

LIAM

I fucking love this. Ivan has an impressive record. He's earned this fight just as I have. He's leaner than I am, well-matched in height and reach, and white as snow, save for the tattoo on his left pec. I've seen a star like that, and it's nagging my brain, but there's no time to think about it now.

"Liam, focus mate that was a banging' round, now keep your guard up, find your opening, and end this. You hear me?" Ronan says, looking me in the eyes.

I nod and stand while everyone files out of the cage. I'm ready to give a show and end this now. The horn blows and we circle each other a few times. He swings and lands a couple of hits. I tilt my head from side to side and see my opening. I step, swinging my left arm, and deliver a strong jab to his face, and before he can recover, I kick him fast and hard to the other side of his face. He hits the ground. Like a lion, I pounce and pummel his face until I feel the ref pull me off and call an end to the fight at 1:34 in the third round. My team goes wild as I sink to my knees, touch the mat, and give silent thanks. I did it. I have my shot now. The crowd is screaming my name. It's so loud in here that I can't hear my thoughts, but I know I need to see her face. I search until our eyes meet with the biggest shit-eating grin on my face, and she radiates pure joy in the smile I'm getting back.

Mr. Gorbachev is clapping and looks pleased too. The ugly fucker, well, he looks pissed, which I'm starting to think is the usual look when it comes to me but fuck it.

SARAH JANE

I walk over to Ivan and attempt to shake his hand and thank him for a great fight, he slaps my hand away. Fair enough, he's mad he lost, I would be in his position. We both walk to the center, standing on either side of the referee, and wait for the announcer. He comes over the PA system and announces:

"At 1 minute 34 seconds into the third round, the referee put a stop to the fight, your winner by TKO is Liam "the lion" O' Conner."

The guys rush me giving me back slaps and cheering. My team and I pose for pictures, I'm so elated at the time I don't realize my Da isn't standing there with us. I answer questions from the commentators about my strategy coming into this fight, walking through each round until the fight was stopped. I know how to be humble, so I make an effort to acknowledge my opponent and his skills. He gave me a run for my money and has my respect. Thanking my sponsor for the opportunity to come here and fight, the crowd, and my team in closing comments. When it's done, we all file out of the octagon to be greeted by Mr. Gorbachev, Anya, and the goons.

"Congratulations, Liam, on your victory. You lived up to your reputation and more. I look forward to our future working relationship," Mr. Gorbachev says.

The way he said it unsettles me, but I return the smile and shake his hand.

"Thank you again for the opportunity, Mr. Gorbachev I look forward to taking home the belt in a few months," I say back.

A look passes over his face but is quickly gone before he nods and exits the auditorium, leaving me with the two

BABA YAGA

goons and Anya. My crew is openly drooling, so I make the introductions ending with Danvers's son, Ronan. He can't help himself and leans in to kiss her hand.

"Lovely to meet such an enchanting woman. I hope Liam wasn't too much of a pain in the arse till we got here."

"Give over, Ronan, you silly git. I've been upstanding since I got here," I say with a quirk of my eyebrow, daring Anya to contradict me.

"Don't worry yourself, Ronan. I can handle Liam and then some. You boys enjoy your victory. I will catch up to you later," she says with the sexiest smirk and then promptly walks away with the goons in tow.

"Liam, mate, I think you're drooling a little. Pick ya jaw up, and let's get to celebrating," Patty says with a slap to my shoulder.

I take one last look at her and then follow the boys out. It's celebrating time.

CHAPTER 11

ANYA

I needed to get away from him at least for a while and needed to be around familiar things I didn't like how off-kilter I was over a stupid man. Watching him fight made me feel like I'd met my equal. He was powerful, determined, and ruthless in what he wanted His smile is infectious and when he looked at me it was like I was the only woman in the room. It's silly and confusing, I'm Anya Gorbachev this behavior is beneath me. Back to business as usual.

I run interference at the front desk where a man is frantic because of a scheduling conflict at the spa for his wife and his mistress who are both on the premises. Bloody idiot.

With that fixed, I walk the casino floors and check in

BABA YAGA

with my dealers and back-room staff. They have eyes on a sleazy-looking gentleman at one of the blackjack tables. Looks like he's counting cards, and the prostitute on his arm has been lifting wallets and jewelry from the nearby players. I notify Dmitry to snag the girl and bring her to the office for a chat, then send Sergei to a stationary position to watch over the sleazy guy until I'm back.

I proceed from the back-room area and meet Dmitry in the hall outside my office. His guest is struggling to get out of the grip he has on her arm, he looks unimpressed as she pulls, and swears demanding she is released. A kick to his shin doesn't faze him but I'm amused. Never ceases to amaze me how dumb people are. I give him a head nod to follow me in, ignoring the death glares from the skank. I walk to my desk and sit down as Dmitry forces her into the chair across from me.

"You'll be emptying that bag of yours on my desk, you will then be vacating this building, and you will not set foot on this property again, or there will be consequences. Be thankful I'm in a pleasant mood today," I say in a manner that refutes any argument.

This five-foot-fuck-all woman that life rode hard, fake as shit, decides to stand up, lay her five-dollar manicure on my pristine desk, and decides opening her mouth is smart.

"Listen here, bitch. I don't know who the fuck you think you are telling me shit; I will not be emptying my bag, and there's nothing you can do about it."

Dmitry moves to grab her; I wave him off with a sweet smile. I look at this defiant little thing. She must need a firmer approach. Maintaining eye contact, I have my hand on a knife, and I pierce it through her hand, nailing it to my desk.

"No, you listen, bitch. I'm someone you don't ever want to meet in a dark corner. I asked nicely. You chose stupidity, so now here we are. You're bleeding on my nice desk, and my patience is thin. Follow my instructions, or you won't be walking when you leave, and you'll be unable to say a word about it. Hard to make money if you can't walk or talk. Take your pick."

She nods while whimpering and trying to free her hand from my desk. I stand, run my fingers down my dress to make sure nothing is out of place, pull my knife out of her hand, and wipe it off on the bar towel to the right of my desk.

"Dmitry, finish up here. Make sure her bag is empty, return the items to their owners and wrap that hand. I don't want blood on my carpet and get this piece of shit off the property."

I turn to her. "Do remember what I told you. I only give one warning. You come back, and a hand will be the least of your problems." I saunter out my door to security to tag her ID and photo in the system.

When I enter the security office, the men on tonight are new, so I ask where Alexey is. They point to the monitor of my room downstairs. I wasn't called to fix anything, so I move around the desk to take a look at what is so captivating. On the monitor, Alexey stands to the side, arms crossed, looking almost disgusted at the events taking place in the middle of the room.

That's when I see the Butcher doing a number on the fighter Liam beat tonight. Ivan looks like he's been worked over well and is barely conscious. Vlad doesn't like defeat of any kind. Ivan's nose is broken, and both eyes are swollen shut. His right arm hangs funny, and it appears Vlad has broken a few fingers as well. Vlad removed his suit jacket and shirt and is standing in what was once a white undershirt. It's covered in Ivan's blood. He's tense, covered in sweat and blood with a look of pure evil on his face as he towers over Ivan. I can't hear what is said but Alexey moves forward to help Ivan, and Vlad looks at the camera as if he somehow knows I'm watching and heads to the exit.

I'm moving to the exit before I even fully realize I'm doing it. I don't want to be anywhere near here when he gets back. I exact judgment for my father. It's my job and I'm very good at it, but Vlad's evil incarnate. He takes and takes, and he gets off on the pain he inflicts. I've heard stories from the girls that Vlad keeps on rotation; even in the bedroom, he's forceful, angry, and cruel. I don't run from anything, but that man I'd make an exception if I knew it would matter.

Back on the casino floor, I find Sergei still on watch. The sleaze ball is counting cards, so I give Sergei the order to remove him and make sure he's aware of the consequences that come with cheating in my father's casino before he escorts him out. With everything under control, for the time being, I find myself heading to the elevator in search of something I have no business looking for.

CHAPTER 12

LIAM

This is how you celebrate! We got dressed up and went out to an amazing steakhouse courtesy of my sponsor, we did shots. I shook hands with so many people I lost count. I signed some T-shirts and took photos. Even signed a pair of big old fake titties. It's surreal. The guys pick up a few women, and we head up to the penthouse for the after-party. I grab a bottle of water to keep hydrated while we drink, nobody likes a hangover, and I don't want to be wasted for the fun.

Pat, or Patty as we like to call him, Ronan, Finn, and Mac have been with me forever. When Danvers took me on at that gym all those years ago, I didn't realize I was not only gaining a second father but also four brothers who would help mold me into the man I am now and follow me into battle, no questions asked. We're close and share all things, even women, from time to time. So it's not unusual that the women shaking their asses and gyrating their hips to the music will have several willing participants. Bunny, with long blond hair, pulled back in a ponytail, tits some sugar daddy must've bought her, and blood-red lips struts over to Patty and bends over at the waist showing off her thong and already wet pussy.

He leans over and tells her, "Hands on the coffee table."

We watch as he runs his hand up her legs, taking the scrap of fabric she calls a dress up to her waist, slides her thong to the side, and proceeds to eat her pussy like it's his last meal.

The brunette with mile-long legs and an ass you could bounce a coin off gets on her knees in front of Finn, who pulls his cock out, and she sucks on it like it's her favorite lollipop. Mac is finger fucking the saucy redhead while Ronan fucks her face. The room is filled with moans, groans, and debauchery. And myself, well I settle in across from them on the couch to watch. I might join in the fun later, but for now, I'm hard just watching my brothers fill every hole they can.

Soon enough, the party breaks up with Bunny leaving with Patty, the brunette with Finn, and Mac, leaving the saucy redhead with green eyes and pouty lips with Ronan and me.

He has her on all fours on the floor in front of me screaming, "Oh god, oh god!" Let me tell you, God is not here.

She grabs onto my legs for support as he rocks into her, and she reaches for my belt.

SARAH JANE

That's when I hear a throat clear, and that voice, which I could listen to all day, says, "You get any closer to that dick, Delayna, and you'll be drinking through a straw in your neck for the rest of your life."

ANYA

Three heads spin to where I'm standing. Liam looks surprised, Delayna knows to be afraid because she works for my father, of course, and Ronan who's still on the floor in front of me, just keeps up a leisurely pace in D's back door with a smirk on his face.

"How delightful to see you again, love," Ronan says so carefreely that I want to punch him in the face as I also try not to smirk.

"Party is over, Ro. Time to take your company and finish up elsewhere, mate," Liam says to him.

He pulls out, tucks himself into his pants, throws D over his shoulder, salutes Liam, and winks at me as he passes by on the way to the door.

Liam hasn't taken his eyes off me as I slowly walk to sit across from him in the vacant chair and cross one leg over the other. He follows every movement with his eyes, and he looks hungry.

"How long were you standing there, Anya?"

"Not long enough, apparently." I lie through my teeth.

I will not tell him I came in shortly after the show

started. I will not tell him I watched from the foyer, reveling in the sinfully delicious display. And I won't ever admit I played with myself, rubbing my clit raw until my release came with his name upon my lips.

I lick my bottom lip slowly and, decision made, I tilt my head to the side and voice the thoughts running rampant in my head.

"Liam come here."

I wait to see if he complies. This is the pivotal moment where two alphas dance to see who comes out on top.

He slowly rises to his feet and saunters over. Before he reaches me, I unfold my legs and plant one high-heeled foot as high on his chest as I can reach.

"Kneel."

He follows the command with an arched brow. I plant both feet on the floor beside him so he's kneeling between my legs.

"Do you want to fuck me, Liam?"

"I want to do more than just fuck you, Anya, and you fucking know it. Don't play games. It's beneath you love," he says as his eyes roam my entire body and back to my mouth.

"You're right. It is, and I always get what I want."

I stand, unclip the halter of my dress, and let it slip to the ground, leaving only my thong, garter, and stilettos.

"Jesus Christ, you are perfect," he whispers as he tries to reach for me. I give his hand a light tap standing before him with my pussy at his eye level. "Take my thong off, Liam."

His rough hands reach for me and slowly pull the string down my leg. He leans in and inhales.

"Are you wet for me, beautiful? Mmmm."

He groans, blowing air on my already wet pussy.

I swing my leg over one shoulder, giving a full view of how wet I am.

"Why don't you find out? And Liam? I'm going to fuck your face now, and I expect an orgasm."

"I think I like you bossy, baby, and don't worry I got you."

He smirks before leaning forward and leisurely licking from back to front, making the most delicious sound before making a full-course meal out of my pussy.

He licks and sucks and nibbles as I hold his head and slowly roll my hips. I can feel my orgasm building. He reaches between us and inserts two fingers with such force that I scream and grab his head harder. Lick, suck, nibble, and thrust, over and over.

"That's it. Mmm. So close. Fuck, fuck, fuck."

I'm moaning, trying to pull away. It's too intense, but he grips me harder, slaps my ass with his free hand, and sucks hard on my clit. I lose it, and I'm falling. I can't catch my breath, and the orgasm won't stop. He licks and licks as I slowly come back to reality. When I finally open my eyes and look down, the pure raging lust in his eyes almost undoes me again.

"My turn," is all I hear before he lifts me from the ground and heads to the bed.

CHAPTER 13

LIAM

I've died and gone to heaven; I must have because there's no way, in reality, I could have just handed my balls to this woman in my arms. I'm not a submissive man, but I will fall to my knees anytime, anywhere this woman ordered me to. When that dress dropped, my jaw went with it. She's flawless, from her porcelain skin, highlighted with beautiful tattoos, to her curves begging to be licked, right down to the prettiest pussy glistening with wetness that fuels that caveman in me. Her tits are amazing too, but I was too distracted by that long, lean leg that she draped over my shoulder and the order that followed. An order I followed with the same passion I have for fighting. That first taste of her almost undid me.

I licked, sucked, and nibbled until she shattered, almost

pulling my hair out in the process. I looked up to watch her face as she slowly came back down. She looked... heck, I don't even have the vocabulary to describe it, but I almost felt bad for ruining the moment. Almost.

"My turn," I growled as I stood and picked her up wrapping her long, beautiful legs, still wearing those fuck-me heels around my waist.

I walk toward the bedroom. She sounds content, and with what I have in mind for tonight, that just won't do, so I stop and shove her against the wall.

She jolts, looking at me with an eyebrow arched. I smirk, lean forward, and take her blood-red lips in mine. She bites down a little, then swipes her tongue along the seam of my lips. I'll take it all, and right now, I want her worked up enough to let me have my way with her.

Our lips both open, and I use my tongue to fuck her mouth the same way I did her pussy minutes before. I'm sure the taste of her cum is still on my tongue, but by the enthusiasm I'm getting from her, I don't think she gives two fucks. I maneuver us into the doorway and ruffle through my gym bag which sits on the chair just inside the door. I grab what I need and walk toward the bed. Anya lands with a slight bounce and leans back on her elbows to watch as I slowly start unbuttoning my shirt.

"Get naked, Liam. We are far past teasing," she says as she slowly spreads her legs.

"Your wish is my command."

I rip the buttons clean from the shirt and undo my dress pants. I can't look away from her as I slowly reveal my throbbing cock from my boxers. Anya slowly smiles- with what I imagine is- appreciation and licks her lips.

BABA YAGA

"This is going to hurt so good, baby."

I lean over, place my hands under her arms, and shift her farther up the bed until she's nestled close enough to the headboard for what I have in mind. I reach back and grab the hand wraps I had grabbed from my bag. Running my hands slowly up her body, I take her hands and push them up above her head. I enclose one wrist through a loop I made with my hand wrap, loop the other end through the headboard, and enclose her other wrist, effectively tying her to my bed and allowing me to enjoy every inch.

"Tut, tut, tut, Liam, this will not hold me, and who knew you had a kinky side?"

"Anya, you have no idea just how kinky I like it, and it's not meant to hold you. Just tell me if you want to be untied. Otherwise, shut that pretty mouth of yours before I fill it."

Her nose flares, but I get no argument. Such a shame, I was kind of hoping for a little rebellion. I slowly take a hard pink nipple between my lips and suck. She gasps and bucks as I move to repeat the same to the other nipple. I'm so hard that if I don't get inside her soon, I'm going to embarrass myself.

I keep sucking on her breast and run my left hand down to slowly rub circles on her clit with my thumb. Anya is thrashing her head back and forth, moaning. I insert two fingers and keep up on her clit. Leaning back on my knees, I keep up the assault on her pussy while giving my cock a good tug, then wipe off the precum with my right thumb. I was smart enough to toss a condom on the bed when I took my pants off, so I rip it open with my teeth, glove up, and move into place. Slowly taking my fingers out of her pussy,

I suck each one, savoring her taste, and line my cock up with her entrance.

"I don't make love, baby. Are you ready? This will be hard and rough."

"God, yes, get inside me," she breathes out between gritted teeth.

"God's not here, Anya," I say as I thrust into her, taking myself a little off guard by how tight she feels clamped around my dick.

I'm above average size, and Anya is suffocating my dick in the best way; I can't hold back.

ANYA

I am not a delicate flower by any means. I kill people. I fuck and move on. I don't beg, I don't allow a man to tie me up, and I certainly don't allow a man to boss me around in the bedroom. There is something inherently freeing about giving up control to Liam, but if he thinks it'll always be this way, he's sorely mistaken.

I can't think straight and haven't been able to since the first orgasm in the living area. Every inch of my body is aware of him, First, it was his mouth and tongue, and now his dick, as he thrusts inside me- it hurts in the most delicious way. This man has obliterated any idea I had about him. My nipples will feel his mouth for days, and I'll be lucky if I can sit right after the pounding my pussy is taking right now.

I can feel my orgasm building, so I wrap my hands

around the restraint holding my wrists to stabilize myself. Wrapping my legs around his waist, I dig my heels into his lower back and let go. I come in waves over and over, moaning Liam's name incoherently.

Liam keeps up the savage pace as his skin glistens with sweat.

I feel so sexy and powerful, wringing every drop of pleasure from my body. When I feel my pussy pulse as another orgasm builds, I make a quick decision. It's my turn to play, so taking the fabric binding my wrists, I use it as an anchor to wrap my right leg around his left, then lock it and buck my hips. Using the momentum, I roll him onto his back. The look on his face says he's in complete shock that I managed to flip him while not only tied up at the wrists but with him still inside me. Before he decides to fight me, I slowly swivel my hips, and his eyes all but roll back in his head.

"You're just full of surprises, beautiful. You feel so fucking good. Ride my cock, baby, make me come," he growls as he grips my hips.

Moving my hips up and down, picking up speed with the help of Liam's hands at my waist, I can feel every inch of his thick cock swelling as he reaches for his orgasm. I move faster and with no finesse. I want this man undone, and I want my name on his lips when it happens.

"Give me what I want, Liam. Come for me now. Fill me up."

With one more thrust of my hips, he roars my name. His cock throbs inside me as his release fills the condom, and my release soon follows.

I collapse on his chest, and he places small kisses on

my head as he reaches up and releases my wrists from the headboard. They hurt, and I'm sure there will be marks tomorrow, but I can't seem to care.

I slide off him to lie on my side as he gives me one more kiss before getting up to deal with the condom. He comes back with a warm cloth, reaching between my legs to clean me up before tossing the cloth on the floor. I don't linger long after sex, but I'm euphoric right now, so I just lie here as Liam lies on his side facing me, looking into my eyes.

"Without sounding like a pussy and a caveman, I'll just say that you own me, woman, and I own you, no point in saying different," he almost whispers as he tucks a strand of my hair behind my ear and slowly looks at the tattoos on my body.

I don't argue as I don't want to ruin the moment. Reality will come crashing down soon enough.

He traces my tattoos with his finger, and I know the second he sees and stops on my brand. The star of the brotherhood, the tattoo given to all Bratva. Mine is slightly different from most as my father is the Pakhan, but the reality is here, and any moment we were having is ruined by the next words from his lips.

"What does this tattoo represent? Ivan had a similar one. It looks familiar, but I can't think of where I've seen it before."

I don't answer. Instead, I get up, walk to the bathroom, steal the robe off the hook on the back of the door, wrap myself in it like armor, and slip my mask back onto my face. I've done this before; I can walk away from him.

BABA YAGA

"You're mistaken, and it's none of your business. Thank you for an entertaining evening, Liam. Goodnight."

I walk straight out of the room and pick up my dress leaving my thong. He can have a souvenir. As I head out the door, Liam scrambles out of bed, calling my name. I ignore it, knowing full well that if I turn around and go back to him, to this man I'll tell him things he has no business knowing and sign his death warrant in the process.

CHAPTER 14

LIAM

What the ever-loving fuck happened? By the time I had hopped up and covered my bare arse to go after Anya, she was long gone. I feel like I have whiplash. One minute, I was balls deep in the woman, then there was cuddling, and I'm not the cuddling type. I asked a question and the amazing sexy deviant disappeared with the ice queen everybody else gets taking her place. I shouldn't be over-thinking this, but my gut is telling me I'm missing something big, and that tattoo has something to do with it. Some shady-ass shit is going on around here, and I don't like being left in the dark. Time to find good old Dad and get some answers.

I pounded on his door for a solid five minutes before I heard him swearing like a sailor and shuffling my way. The door swings open, and I know in my bones that shit has officially hit the fan. My father looks like death warmed over and smells like he bathed in whatever poison he was inhaling last night.

"Liam, my boy, congrats on the fight. How was celebrating last night?" he says with a mild slur.

"Jesus Christ, Da. Are you still drunk? You'd think you won a fight last night," I say, pushing my way into his room.

It looks like he cleaned out the mini bar three times over already, and empty bottles, pizza boxes, and clothes are thrown all over.

I take a seat in an open spot on the couch and look at my father, a really good look at him, and I feel like the floor is falling out from beneath me.

"Da, I need you to answer a few questions for me, and for once, I need you to be honest. Who is Anatoli Gorbachev, and what exactly has he promised you for me?"

"He's a businessman, Liam," he says too quickly.

"I said no lying, Da. We both know he's more than just a businessman, and I want to know what you've gotten me into."

I'm trying to keep my temper under control, but I know something isn't right, I haven't since that first handshake with the man. Declan O' Conner has a tell when lying and deflects in the worse way, so I know he's working up to feeding me a load of bullshit.

"Honestly, Liam." He's getting angry now as he struggles to stand in front of me, pointing his beefy finger in my face. "You see threats where there are none. He's a businessman who approached me and offered you a shot at a title match, don't mess this up for us, Liam. To toe the line and do what you do best, stick to fighting. I handle the business."

"Us? Us? There is no us in this, Da. I'm getting really tired of you taking credit for shit you have no real part of. It's my blood, my sweat, my hard work that has kept you in this lifestyle that you feel so fucking entitled to. If you're going to keep bullshitting me, I'll find out the truth for myself. Stay out of my way, or you'll find yourself having to look for a new meal ticket." I'm on my feet and heading to the door before I do something I regret.

"Liam, I may be a fuck up, and lord knows I've failed as a father but listen to me when I say you're barking up the wrong tree. Leave this be" he says, grabbing my arm.

I'm so mad I shake him off with more force than I intended, and he falls back, hitting the glass coffee table with a crash.

Glass goes everywhere, Dad's eyes are closed, and there's blood starting to soak the floor. I'm shaking and frozen, just looking at the shadow of a good man bleeding on the floor.

We must've made a racket because fists start pounding on the door, knocking me out of my trance. Ronan is yelling my name and telling Patty to kick the door in. I quickly move to the door and swing it open, and my mates all pile in, eyes bugged out, taking in the space and finally landing on dad.

Finn and Mac run to Dad while Ronan grabs my arms "What the fuck happened, Liam?"

He's shaking me. I know I should answer, but I can't. I'm just staring as Finn barks orders at Patty to grab towels,

Baba Yaga

and Mac helps him roll Dad over to find where the blood is coming from.

"Snap the hell out of it!"

Ronan slaps me like the bitch I'm acting like. I blink, and the look of concern on my brother's face forces me to rein in my shit.

"I'm here, Ro. Thanks. It was an accident. He was pissed because I asked him some questions that, of course, he dodged. I tried to leave 'cause I was boiling over, and he grabbed my arm. I didn't mean to shove him so hard. I just wanted him to let go, and then he fell. I just wanted him to let go." I'm rambling, I know I am. I just keep repeating it.

"It's okay. Stay here for a second. I'm going to go check on Declan, and see what's up," he says before walking over and kneeling beside Finn.

Finn is a paramedic back home; he's running through the injuries he sees but says the main concern is how hard Dad hit his head while intoxicated. His pulse is thready, and he hasn't come to yet.

I'm moving to the phone by the bed, and on instinct, I pick up and call the one person I probably shouldn't but need the most.

"Anya, I need you now, come to my dad's suite, and hurry."

––––––––

ANYA

"Anya, I need you now, come to my dad's suite, and hurry," is all I hear from Liam before he hangs up.

I look up, and everyone in the morning meeting is looking at me, including my father and Vlad.

"What is it, Anya? I thought I made it clear no phones in my meetings," he says in that tone most shrink back from.

Vlad sits to his right; I can feel his eyes boring into my head. I don't acknowledge him. Instead, I stand and nod my head in respect to my father.

"I have to go," I say and walk out.

Once the door closes, I run to the elevators right past Alexey, who falls in step, keeping up the pace.

Out of all my father's men, Alexey is the closest thing to my friend. I mean that loosely, but we grew up together in the Bratva, so it's bred into us, the loyalty and ruthlessness it takes to be in the brotherhood. I had always hoped my father would've picked Alexey to give my hand to. He would at least stand at my side and take orders. My father, however, picked the Butcher leaving me feeling like my life will have a short shelf life if I don't learn obedience.

Once we get in the elevator, Alexey gives me a side-eye. He's not asking what's wrong, he knows I don't get agitated, nor do I run for anything, so it must be serious. The doors open, and we run to Declan's suite.

It's pure chaos. Liam is pacing, Ronan is standing beside Patty, and they're both looking at the other two men kneeling beside Declan. He's bleeding and unconscious. Finn is stuffing towels underneath his back to stop the bleeding while Mac checks his pulse. What the hell happened here?

BABA YAGA

This is familiar, though. I can handle this, so I remove my leather jacket and look at Alexey, giving him a nod. He moves to the phone and rings for our in-house doctor. We have one on staff for all manner of things. He's discreet and well-funded. I need to get everyone under control, so I whistle loud, and the five men swivel to the two people they hadn't seen arrive.

"Listen up! Liam, sit the fuck down before you put a hole in the carpet. Ronan, go to the elevator and wait with Alexey for the doctor to arrive. Finn, give me a sitrep about his condition, and Mac get me a shot of vodka."

Nothing.

"Move!" I yell, and boy, do they get going.

"Declan is bleeding from a deep cut in his midback. No major arteries hit, but he's lost a lot of blood. Minor contusions all over and several cuts from the table, some will need stitches. My major concern is his head. Liam said he was intoxicated when he fell, and I don't know if there is swelling. His pulse is steady but weak, and he hasn't come to, so he needs an ambulance and scans," Finn rattles off to me as Mac hands me a shot, and I fling it back.

I'm just about to respond when I hear Alexey behind me with a gurney and the doctor in tow. I repeat what Finn told me, and the doctor has the men assist him in getting Declan on the gurney. He checks his pulse and opens each eye to shine a light, checking for a response.

"Мне нужно доставить его вниз Аня, ему нужно сканирование, переливание крови и швы. Я возьму Алексея, чтобы сохранить остальных здесь" *(I need to get him downstairs, Anya. He needs a scan, a blood trans-*

fusion, and stitches. I'll take Alexey keep the others here.) Victor says in his usual no-nonsense manner.

I nod and turn to lay into Liam and his friends. I don't take any pleasure in doing this, but they can't follow him; it'll lead to too many questions. Alexey and Victor wheel Declan toward the elevator with Victor spouting instructions in Russian to whoever is on call downstairs. Liam and Ronan move to follow, and I block their path.

"You stay here. He's in the best hands, and I want to know exactly what the hell happened in here before my father gets alerted to this situation." I brook no argument, and Liam sinks back onto the couch.

Ronan moves to help the three other men start cleaning up. I'll get the cleaners up here after I get the information.

"Liam, look at me and tell me what happened here."

He can't meet my eyes; at this moment, he looks like a boy waiting for punishment.

He starts slow, but events seem to be out of order. I manage to gather they fought, and Liam tried to leave when Declan grabbed him. Liam shook him off, and Declan fell.

It sounds like an accident, but when I push to find out what they fought about, Liam looks at Ronan, who gives a slight shake of his head. So that tells me two things. One, the argument had something to do with me, and two we might have a problem. I don't understand how I can be his first call yet be kept in the dark. On the other hand, I can't allow him to dig or bring attention to himself. My father will smudge him from existence- investment or not- if he thinks Liam is a problem.

"Gentlemen, please take Liam back to his suite. I'll get cleaners to rid the room of the mess. Get cleaned up. I'll

BABA YAGA

check on Declan and report back to you within the hour." I dare them to contradict me.

"Thank you, Anya, for coming when I called. Please make sure my father is okay." He leans in, places a soft kiss on my lips, and leaves followed by all the guys.

Each gives me a nod of acknowledgment except Ronan, who stops, waiting for everyone to leave. Standing at 6'2", I'd wager, with dark- red hair and bright green eyes, he's quite attractive. I don't appreciate the look I'm getting, though.

"He cares for you, Anya, and whatever the hell Declan has got him mixed up in, I want to be undone. If you feel anything for my friend, fix it. I won't see him hurt, and I'll go to war with anyone who dares. Do we understand each other?"

"I appreciate your loyalty, I do, Ronan. I'm not privy to my father's business dealings, but I'll give you a little advice as well. I care about him too, so he needs to stop asking questions. Nothing good will come of it, if you catch my drift," I say as sweetly as possible. "One more thing, Ronan, don't ever threaten me again. Looks are deceiving," are my parting words as I leave.

I push the elevator button for the main floor, hoping for an update on Declan. When the doors open to the ground floor, I'm met by The Butcher. Fuck.

CHAPTER 15

ANYA

"Come with me, princess. Your father is waiting," Vlad says with a smugness I wish I was strong enough to wipe from his mouth.

"I don't need a babysitter or an escort, Butcher. I know the way," I say as I try to walk past him.

He roughly grabs my arm and leans in to growl in my ear, "I don't think you quite understand who is in charge here, Anya, but you will, one day, real soon. You will understand it very well."

He doesn't release my arm as he turns us toward my father's office and starts walking. I quicken my pace to keep up with his long strides, and every possible situation runs through my head as to why I'm being accosted. Vlad doesn't wait for Dmitry to open the door for us or acknowl-

BABA YAGA

edge the look Dmitry gives him for having his hands on me before he pushes into the office and forces me into the chair across from my father. I can't tell what my father is thinking or why the Butcher is pacing behind me with that look he gets when he wants to break something.

"Vlad, sit your ass down or leave. Take your pick," my father says before turning to look at me. "It seems to me, Anya, that you didn't understand the assignment I gave you," he starts. I go to interject, but he holds a hand up. "No, you will listen and not open your mouth. I told you to pick this boy up, show him around, and make sure he gets to the appropriate places at the appropriate times. I, however, did not permit you to fuck him, railroad my plans, and from what I've just heard from Alexey and Victor, allow Liam to get curious and make a fucking mess. Now, I give you a lot of grace, my daughter, but don't mistake my love for leniency. What the fuck happened? And if your answer doesn't appease me, I will find somebody else to do the job you obviously can't." Long-winded and irate would be an accurate evaluation of my father's mood.

How fucking dare, someone watch and spy on me. When I find out who it was, they won't like it. Now I see why Vlad is so pissed. He sees me as his property. Up to this point, discretion in the bedroom has been key to my happiness. The rat will pay for this as well.

"Well, father, I'm sorry you feel I haven't done the job to your satisfaction. I wasn't aware whom I fuck was anybody's business. I have shown him around, he made all his commitments, and I have prevented all situations that arose where questions might be asked. With regards to this morning, I don't see how I could have prevented what

SARAH JANE

happened." I think I'm being smart here, but I quickly realize I'm not when my father, despite being up in years, reaches across his desk and grabs my face.

"Don't you fucking forget who you're talking to Anya. Show me some respect, or I will cut your fucking tongue out myself. Am I understood?"

I manage a nod, and he releases my chin. Whatever plan my father has for Liam must be important for him to treat me like I'm still a child. I've racked my brain thinking of what it could be. I'm not seeing the bigger picture somehow. What would he need with a fighter? My thoughts are interrupted by Vlad asking to take over and do a better job than I have. *Over my dead body.*

"I've got this under control, Father. There was no way I could account for a family disturbance this morning. From all accounts, it was an accident, a heated argument that ended with Declan injured after trying to prevent his son from leaving." I go for a slightly bored tone to mask this sick feeling I have in my gut that I'm the one in the dark.

"What do you think the argument was about, you stupid bitch?" Vlad spits at me. "We have eyes on that dumb fuck twenty-four hours a day, so we saw and heard all this morning's events. I especially love the conversation at the end between you and the red-headed friend of his. You care for this fighter, which was your first mistake, Anya. He's a mark, a job. Maybe you need to be reminded where your loyalties should be?" he says with lust in his eyes. He would love to get his hands on me. Pain is his foreplay.

"Vlad, that's enough. I think you are forgetting the chain of command here. That 'bitch' is still my child and

BABA YAGA

the heir to my seat. Leave us. I would like a word alone with my daughter."

Vlad is seething because he's being dismissed and reminded of where he stands in the pecking order. He nods and walks out, slamming the door behind him. If my father didn't still need Liam, I'd be very worried right now for his safety. I look back at my father, who is staring at me with such intensity I feel like he can see my soul.

"Don't make me send Vlad to teach you the consequences of defying me, daughter. I'll take no pleasure in it, but I will do it. You don't get to where I am by being sentimental, Anya. You hand your soul to the devil in this life, there is no going back. You don't leave this life. It's forever. Even in death, the brotherhood comes first. There is no normal for you, Anya. There is no white picket fence for the heir to my seat, so you need to dispense with any thoughts of it. You are Baba Yaga, the boogeyman I send to snuff out anyone in my way. He doesn't know who you are, and he is not made for this life. You will go check on Declan's condition and then report to Liam that his father is on the mend, and has been offered a job here in event promotions, so he won't be going back to Ireland with them. You are to have them on a flight back tomorrow, and I don't want to hear back otherwise."

"Yes, father" I stand and walk to the door.

"And if you are going to spread your legs like a common whore, I can hand you over to Alexey and at least make money off you," are my father's parting words as I leave.

This is fucking bad. Real fucking bad. I stop by the security office where Sergei, Dmitry, and Alexey are

79

briefing the next security shift. I interrupt by throwing a walkie at the wall. Heads swivel, guns are drawn, and I suddenly have everyone's attention. I smile, withdraw a knife from my custom belt holster I had made for when I'm not wearing a dress, and slowly start tapping my chin with it. I saunter around the office, making sure to lightly brush my knife along each chest before standing in front of Alexey.

"When I find out which one of you is the rat reporting back to the Butcher and my father about my whereabouts, we will have a conversation you won't like the outcome of. You fucks seem to forget that even though my father is in charge, I'm the one who hands down justice. I'm the one in the shadows painting the walls red with the very knife I hold in my hand. Be sure to remember that, or Baba Yaga will be visiting you while you sleep."

I give Alexey a tap on the chin with my knife and make eye contact with each man. They all stand a little taller showing visible reactions to my threat.

"Have a good evening, gentleman," I say sweetly before exiting through the back to see Victor in his medical office and get an update on Declan.

CHAPTER 16

LIAM

I'm losing my mind waiting for word about my dad. I never meant to hurt him. I've run it over and over in my head, wondering how it could have gone better; if I hadn't pushed so hard to get answers. His reaction is proof I hit a button. We're flying home tomorrow to start training camp for my title shot in six months, so I'll have the flight to finesse the answers out of him. Can't avoid me 30,000 feet in the air.

Thoughts of Anya flit in and out of my head. I've always been honest about who and what I am. My goals and dreams have driven me for as long as I can remember, yet two days ago, a siren walked into my world, and I'm ready to walk off a short pier for her. She's strong and sharp-tongued, and watching her spar with such grace had me in awe. But the moment I knew I was gone was at

SARAH JANE

dinner when her smile lit up her face and her laughter filled the silence. Having her watch me fight made me think how great it would be to have her in my corner. Her take-charge attitude earlier when I called for help was sexy as fuck.

She sees me. I feel seen and respected. We are equals, and I want, hell, I don't know what I want. These thoughts make me anxious, and the stress of fighting with my father has me wound up. I'm formulating a plan when I hear a knock on the door, followed by Anya walking in. I'm up and moving toward her as soon as I see the cold look on her face.

"Is my father okay? Why did it take you so long to get back up here? Can I see him?" I'm peppering her with questions.

"Liam, take a breath. I just came from seeing the doctor, and your father is stable and expected to make a full recovery."

"Oh, thank god. You scared me for a second when you came in with that look on your face," I say before she cuts me off.

"I'm not finished. He required stitches in several places, a blood transfusion, and a CT scan to make sure there was no swelling in his brain. He was intoxicated still from his toxicology report, which is why it took so long for him to come to."

"But he will recover, right? Do I need to change our flight tomorrow until he feels better and is cleared to fly" I'm so relieved he's going to be ok I almost missed the look Anya gives before she slips the mask back on that she is so good at hiding behind.

"He won't be flying home to Ireland with you, Liam.

BABA YAGA

My father offered him a job, and he took it, which is why he was celebrating last night. He will be doing event promotions here at the resort." She looks like she has a bad taste in her mouth before she cuts me at the knee. "I thought you'd be happy. No more taking care of him or cleaning up his messes. He won't have to be in your shadow anymore begging for scraps."

"How fucking dare you say that shit to me, Anya. You met me forty-eight hours ago, you know nothing about my life or his. Do you think one dinner and a roll in the hay with me makes you an expert? I want to hear this from his mouth, not yours."

"That won't be possible. The doctor doesn't want anything or anyone that might cause him to stress near him right now. It is what it is, Liam. Enjoy your last night here and I'll be by in the morning to make sure you make your flight," she says indifferently before turning around and walking back out the door.

Something happened this morning to make her so cold. I'm not done with this conversation, so I barrel out the door after her, sticking my hand in the elevator door just in time to stop it from closing.

"I have nothing else to say to you, Liam. Get your hand out of the door."

The doors open back up, and I walk in. Once they shut, I hit the emergency stop button, preventing us from going anywhere until I'm good and ready.

"I'm not fucking finished with you yet," I growl as I back her into the back wall.

"That's too bad because I'm done with you," she says before sliding around me to head for the release button.

83

This woman makes me a fucking caveman. I blindly react and grab her around the back of the neck, holding her firmly before pressing my chest to her back. "I said I'm not finished with you yet, Anya."

She responds with a sharp elbow to my side, catching me off guard, so I release her neck. She swivels and uses her right leg to kick me, narrowly missing my balls. Game on, beautiful. We go back and forth, grappling with her trying to get to the elevator door. She's going full tilt on me, leaving me wondering how and why she learned to fight this way. I get a good left hook to my mouth causing my lip to bleed. All bets are off now. I charge her, lifting her clear off the floor, and slam her back into the elevator wall.

"Submit to me, Anya."

"Fuck you, Liam." She struggles to get loose.

"Fuck me? You will don't worry," I say before taking her mouth.

I'm running on pure lustful anger. I pin her to the wall with one arm under her ass and my chest against hers.

Running my free hand up her legs to the button on her jeans, I pause long enough to say, "tell me to stop. If you don't want to be fucked tell me now, Anya, before I lose all sense of control."

"You talk too much. Shut up and fuck me," she breathes out between kisses.

She licks along my bottom lip where I'm bleeding before kissing me so thoroughly that I lose all reason. I have her button popped in two seconds flat, and I'm yanking down her pants while she attempts to get closer. I

BABA YAGA

release her to the ground, spin her around, and bend her at the waist so that her perfect ass is facing me.

"Hold the railing, baby."

She stalls in taking my order, so I raise my right hand and smack her ass, leaving a mark on her porcelain skin. She jolts and lets out a gasp but pushes her ass back toward me. I take my left hand and repeat the same to the other side, so now she has matching marks. I keep going until she's moaning with each smack. I can see her pussy dripping, so I give her two more smacks before releasing my cock and driving into her so hard she hits her head. She moans and purrs like a cat before pushing back toward my pelvis to match each thrust. The elevator is filled with my grunts, her moans, which are words I can't make out, and the slapping of my balls on the back of her thighs. I take her long hair at the nape of her neck and wrap it around my fist, pulling slightly as I take all this frustration and anger out on her pussy. My balls start to tighten, but there's no way I'm finishing alone, so I pull her head back to suck on her neck while my other hand curls around her front to rub hard circles on her clit.

"Come for me, Anya, now," I growl before pinching her clit hard, sending her over the edge.

I follow after her, growling and bucking up against her ass until I've emptied every last drop I have left into her. Reality crashes in when I pull out and realize I didn't wear a condom as cum leaks from her pussy. I rip my shirt over my head and clean her up best I can before pulling up her jeans. She does her pants up and turns to look at me. Her mask is slipping, I can see it. I cup her face and kiss her as tenderly as I can muster. The elevator pings, indicating she released the emergency button. The doors open, and she pulls away.

"Goodbye, Liam."

She slips out the doors before they close, and I'm left in the elevator, holding a shirt full of my cum with my dick hanging out.

Chapter 17

Anya

I feel sick to my stomach walking away the way I did, but I knew going into this it would have an expiration date. The look on his face as I said goodbye after letting him purge all his anger into my body was the first time in my entire life I felt regret. There's a pain in my chest and a rock in my stomach as I head to the stairs. I figure I'll take the stairs to the next floor, and once I know Liam is gone, I can hop on an elevator. A key card is needed to access the stairs to the penthouse, so I won't run into anyone till I exit the private stairs to the public floors, which is a small blessing. I don't understand these feelings coursing through me, and I need to process them. My body is wound tight, I need a distraction from this mess I've gotten myself into. Anatoli is not a man I ever thought I would disappoint. I can't figure out why I would do it now. Why him? Why am I not mad at myself?

Liam fills my head like a slideshow from the first look to laughing with him at dinner to watching him fight to our night together. Everything replays over and over, and when it settles back on that last look, my smile fades and that horrible feeling makes its home in my gut.

I've just accessed the first public floor from the penthouse, which happens to be Declan's floor, so I let myself in and do a quick inspection, making sure no evidence was left behind from this morning's event. Satisfied with the skills of our cleaners, I leave. Just as I push the elevator call button, my cell phone buzzes in my back pocket.

"Yes," I answer. It's Alexey with an interesting job for Baba Yaga tonight.

"I'm on my way," I say before hanging up and entering the elevator.

Once I reach the main floor, I turn right and head to the back offices. Walking past the security office, I look in to see who is on duty and notice the two from earlier. I nod, and neither is too keen to look me in the eye, but they both nod. I keep going till I'm in my office. Closing the door behind me, I head across the carpet to the far wall behind my desk, pushing the small panel inward to enter the code required to release the hidden door to my playroom. I take the stairs down and enter 'The Room of Death.' Alexey and Dmitry are holding a man in a crisp black suit with a short, cropped haircut, and reeking of self-righteousness.

A fed, interesting, I muse.

My father doesn't usually touch law enforcement. He owns most of the highest chains of command near and

BABA YAGA

far, so whatever this man did must've been bad to earn a date with me. Alexey hands me the guy's wallet and a burner- like what we use- just as my phone notifies me of an incoming text. I open the screen and read my instructions.

> .... Find out who he's been talking to. I want names and how much he told them. I want him to fully understand the consequences of being a rat before you kill him.

I delete the message after reading it and I'll have my phone "cleaned" after I'm done. Now onto the main event.

I flip open this guy's wallet and take a glance at his picture. Not a bad-looking guy to be fair, but incredibly stupid apparently. Getting his name, I toss his wallet and phone on the table.

I call over my shoulder as I peruse my toys, "Gentleman, please remove the top half of Brian's clothing and hang him up on the roulette wheel."

I can hear both men snicker as clothing is being ripped. Up till now, the FBI agent was quiet, but now he's getting disgruntled and chatty.

"What the fuck is going on? Why am I here? Who are you people?" he yells, and when no answer comes, he struggles harder. "Do you know who the fuck I am? It's life in prison for assaulting a federal agent."

His struggles are futile with Alexey and Dmitry holding

SARAH JANE

him. But I've got to give the man a little respect for trying, despite it doing little to save him.

I'm pretending like I can't decide what tool I'm going to use first when I hear the buckles on the straps connected to the roulette wheel tighten. Brian, whatever his last name is, has nowhere to go.

"Dmitry, come here," I order.

He approaches me on the left, and I hand him a sledge-hammer. "Take this and stand where he can see it."

He nods and returns to stand in front and to the side of Brian, so he's clearly seen but not a threat. . . yet.

My trusty kunai knives are lined up on the table in two thigh holsters. I pick them up and take my time strapping them to each thigh. Rolling up my sleeves, I grab a pair of pliers and tuck them into the back pocket of my jeans. Turning around, I get a look at my plaything all trussed up for the evening.

I usually change into my uniform, so to speak, but these clothes will be a constant reminder of today, so I'll wash them in blood and burn them with the body. It's showtime, and I have a lot of tension to work through.

"Brian, is it? You are here tonight because you've been running your mouth."

"I don't know what you're talking about," he says but judging by the sweat collecting on his upper lip and his forehead, he has an inkling of what I'm talking about.

"Don't interrupt me again, Brian."

I nod to Alexey who gives him a hard punch to his right kidney. Brian lets out a pained grunt, closing his eyes briefly before looking back up at me.

BABA YAGA

"You can do whatever you want to me, but I don't know anything," he wheezes out.

"I was so hoping you'd say that Brian. Now we get to play a game. I will ask you a question, and if you answer truthfully, I'll let Alexey here handle your punishment. If I feel you are lying, my associate is going to spin that wheel, and I'm going to play with my knives here." To emphasize my point, I tap a long painted nail against the knives on my right leg.

"First question, who ordered you to look into and gain information on Anatoli Gorbachev?"

His eyes give him away, not quite meeting mine; he's worried now. "I don't know who Anatoli Gorbachev is."

I let out a short laugh, causing him to pale further. "That's your first lie, Brian. Spin the wheel, Alexey."

I do love the clicking sounds my wheel makes as Alexey swings toward Dmitry before bringing it back toward him at a clipped pace.

Click, click, click. As the wheel makes its first turn, I pull my first knife out, give Brian a wink as he's coming back around, and let my knife fly. I don't want to cause too much damage yet, but I need to make a point, so I aim right beside his face. He screams as the knife nicks his cheek, severing the bottom of his ear lobe and embedding it in the wood.

"You must not have heard me I do hope that helps. Do I need to repeat the question?" I say, pulling another knife from the holster.

"You crazy, bitch! I told you I don't know anything," he says between clenched teeth.

"Alexey, again. And, Brian, before I sever your other

ear, let me introduce myself, just to give you an idea of how truly fucked you are. My name is Baba Yaga. Judging by the color draining from your face right now you know that name. Good."

The wheel spins again, and I let my knife fly, severing his other ear and into the wood with a thud. Alexey rights him again.

"So now that I have your undivided attention, and hoping those ears are working better now, who sent you to spy on Anatoli?"

"I told you I don't know an Anatoli. I was sent down here to tail a businessman the bureau thought was in bed with the Russians."

Well, that's a start. I give Alexey a nod, and he lands another punch to Brian's kidney. I pull another knife from my holster and ask my next question.

"I think that was the first truthful thing you've said so far. Now, what was this businessman's name, who was the Russian he was supposed to be meeting, and what exactly were your orders?"

"I can't tell you that. I've told you everything I can. I don't know anymore I'll keep my mouth shut if you just let me go now."

Brian clearly doesn't understand that he's not leaving this room alive. I give the order to spin, and the routine repeats four more times, with Brian still claiming he knows nothing. I've pierced both hands, and he's sporting a knife in each thigh, dripping blood all over my floor. I repeat the question again as I grab another knife.

"Ok, ok, the man's name is Kolinski. He gained attention for his not-so-legal dealings in LA involving underage girls and his frequent visits to this casino in Vegas called The Vice. He came like clockwork several times a month. We investigated his financials and noticed cash flowing in and out at irregular amounts but no obvious job to account for how he was paying for his lifestyle."

"He was going to a casino Brian. Of course, cash flow would be irregular as he gambles."

"Yes, that is true, but the amounts he was spending compared to bringing in didn't match. He was also receiving regular payouts from that same casino with no record of a job or services rendered on paper. We had men on him upon his return to LA, but nobody could find or explain the payouts, so this last trip down here, I was sent to follow him."

His breaths are labored as he loses blood. I better speed this up before he kicks the bucket. This complicates things. Fucking Kolinski. As a reward, if you can call it that, for telling the truth, I let Alexey use him as a punching bag as I feign boredom, cleaning under my nail with my knife as I ponder what's missing from the story he's spinning.

Kolinski came here to gamble and fuck girls. I watched him bleed to death staring at his dick, which I cut off not two feet from where I'm standing.

"That's enough, Alexey. Now, Brian, let's continue. You followed this Kolinski to Vegas. What did you find out while following this man, and whom did he meet while here?"

He's struggling to breathe with the few broken ribs he's now sporting, and he sounds defeated as he continues, "At first, nothing happened. He arrived at the casino I mentioned, checked in, and proceeded to his room. I sat in

SARAH JANE

the lobby till he came back down about an hour later headed and straight to the casino. I hung back as he racked up quite a tally, not lucky, I guess. A guy walked toward him that looked like that one." He tilts his head at Dmitry still standing there with the sledgehammer, looking left out if I'm quite honest. "I followed at a distance until he went down a hallway of offices, and I couldn't follow without giving myself away. I peeked around the corner in time and saw this giant motherfucker who looked quite displeased with my guy come out of a room, hold the door open, and all three men disappeared, closing the door behind them."

"And then what, Brian? Did you call anyone? What happened next?" I say, getting impatient and pissed off.

Once again, things are being kept from me. So, Sergei, Dmitry's brother- Brian must see the family resemblance- took Kolinski to Vlad. What did they talk about, and what business did that limp dick fuck have here?

"I waited to update my boss until I had more information. Kolinski came out about twenty minutes later and proceeded to The Kitty House in the resort. I'd guess he's a member by the way the front desk chick acknowledged him. She didn't seem to like him much, but she picked up a phone, spoke into it, hung up a few moments later, and he disappeared down a hallway to get his rocks off."

Get his rocks off? That fucker hurt my friend. I'm about to boil over, but I need more answers. "Did you see him again after that?"

Brian is starting to bleed from his mouth. Internal injuries are a bitch, and his head is swinging as he fights to stay conscious. That just won't do.

BABA YAGA

"Dmitry, if you please, Brian, is trying to sleep, and we need him awake."

Dmitry steps forward and swings the sledgehammer obliterating Brian's left kneecap.

"AAAAAAAAAAA stop, stop, please stop! I'm talking," he begs, coughing up more blood and struggling with each breath.

"I saw him for all of two minutes after a commotion inside the Kitty parlor broke out. A couple of goons in security uniforms came running, followed by a guy in a medical coat. A minute went by, and the doctor came out, followed by one of the security guys carrying a girl that looked like someone used her for a punching bag. They disappeared down another hallway, and the second security guy came out with a bloody Kolinski and this guy." He looks at Alexey.

Are you fucking kidding me? What the hell is going on here? I look at Alexey. "You and I will be having a conversation when we are done."

I look back at Brian, and he's fading fast.

"Almost there, Brian. What happened after Kolinski left with my associate here?"

"Nothing happened. I lost them somewhere. Kolinski never came back to his room. I reported back to my boss, and he said to sit tight until he appeared again. It's been almost forty-eight hours. Wherever he is, I have a feeling I'm going to be joining him shortly."

"Last question, Brian. Who's your boss, and does anyone else know what you told him?"

"I only reported to him, and my boss's name is-"

Before he can say a name Vlad appears with a 9mm Glock and puts a bullet right between Brian's eyes.

I don't think, I just react, spinning and throwing a knife without thinking of the consequences of my actions. I hit the Butcher in his shoulder, causing him to drop the gun.

"Don't ever fucking come in and interfere with my work again, Butcher, or what you just got will be the least of your problems."

I'm vibrating from head to toe with pure adrenaline and anger. I was getting the answers I needed, and whether Vlad knows it or not, he's just fucked up. My father will be furious he interfered. What was Vlad so worried Brian would tell me? I don't believe in coincidences, period. It wasn't just chance that he was there at that moment and ended my interrogation before I got a name. A trip to the security office will tell me just how long the Butcher was listening.

I'm drawn out of my thoughts by Vlad grunting as he pulls my knife from his shoulder, tosses it on the floor, and heads straight for me. I pull two more knives and get into position.

"That's the only time you will ever draw blood from me, Printsessa. Your father won't be around forever to protect you, and when that day comes, I will fucking break you in ways even the great Baba Yaga can't imagine." He stops just shy of my arm's reach and smirks.

"Maybe you need a little taste."

He has that gleam in his eyes as he removes his suit jacket and throws it to the side.

His crisp white shirt is turning red from his wound, and I can just see through the hole in his shirt. Is it too much to

BABA YAGA

ask him to bleed to death now? Probably. My bravado is starting to wane, and he looks like he's just getting started, bleeding or not. *Let's dance then, Butcher.*

We circle each other. I take a few swipes at him with my knives, but he dodges. He swings, narrowly missing my face, and when he tries to sneak in a cheap shot to my side, his fist meets Alexey's instead. By the sharp exhale Alexey makes, I have no doubt I would've been coughing up blood.

"Enough, both of you. Vlad, you and I both know what will happen if you touch the Pakhan's daughter without permission." Looking back at me, he continues, "Anya, don't make this any worse. Walk away now. Dmitry and I will handle the clean-up. Report to your father after you clean up." His eyes are pleading with me, which breaks through my fog of anger.

I lower my knives, nod, and start for the door. I make it to the door before I hear a commotion and Alexey yells "Anja" in a warning. I turn as one of my knives flies past and hits the door with a loud thud. Alexey and Dmitry are holding Vlad, who looks like he's foaming at the mouth because he missed. And because I'm a glutton for punishment, I look at my knife before pulling it out of the door and turning back to Vlad.

"Looks like you're losing your touch, Butcher."

Smiling, I walk out the door as he lets out a roar. *Liam isn't the only one whose days are numbered*, is the last thought I have as I enter my office to shower off the stench death carries. Too bad it doesn't wash off the soul the same way.

CHAPTER 18

ANYA

After a hot shower that would rival the fires of hell and scrubbing myself raw, the adrenaline has worn off, and today's events catch up with me. I wipe the steam off the mirror in my office bathroom, trying to recognize the person looking back at me. In a matter of days, I have disappointed and disobeyed my father, got involved with a man I knew I shouldn't, and made an enemy of the butcher. His revenge will not be swift, and I've never felt so free or more alive. A lesser person would be scared shitless right about now, but they don't call me the boogeyman for nothing.

I wash my face and reapply my makeup. Pulling my hair back, I slowly begin to braid my hair. When done, I tie

BABA YAGA

it off and let it fall down my back. Pulling a fresh pair of jeans, bra, and T-shirt from my closet, I get dressed before bagging up all the bloody garments from earlier and placing them in a garbage bag. I make sure no evidence is left anywhere, walk back to my desk, and grab my phone.

I managed to grab the FBI agent's phone and slip it into my pocket without anyone noticing, so I put it in the safe behind my vanity mirror in the bathroom. One of the girls at The Kitty House is a computer genius and owes me a favor. I'll get her to poke around to find out who he was talking to and maybe get the answers Vlad prevented me from getting. With the plan in place, I head to the security office, handing off the garbage bag for disposal and handing my phone over to be scrubbed. It takes but a few minutes, and I'm handed back my phone with a new SIM card. Bolstering my spine for my conversation with my father, I head to his office and knock on the big door.

"Enter" I hear before I walk in and see Anatoli sitting in a gold lounge chair, I'm sure cost thousands, having a few afternoon shots of vodka. I make it over to the bar waiting for a moment for his permission to drink, he nods, and I make myself a stiff drink. I'm sore from Liam, which feels delicious along with the aftereffects of what happened downstairs I need this drink to brace myself for this conversation. Telling my father what I learned from the fed, plus my suspicions can go sideways if I don't approach it the right way. Vlad has been his right hand for years and up until today, I never would've questioned his loyalty even if I don't like him, but my gut is telling me there is a reason he pulled that trigger before I got what I needed. So, I take

99

a healthy swig of my drink give myself some liquid courage and sit down.

I start with the events after I left his office when I spoke to Victor, and then I relay both Victor had to say, and Declan's new position to Liam.

"He's not happy, but he didn't argue or push too hard," I say between sips.

I then relay the events that occurred downstairs and the information I gathered. I pause to let him mull it over.

"What aren't you telling me, Anya, I know there's more to this report," my father says as he leans back, placing his elbows on the arms of his chair and steepling his fingers with the two forefingers resting under his chin.

I never truly looked at my father. He's always been almost God-like to me, invincible even, but as I try to find the right words to continue, I find myself looking now. He is just over six feet, and even at his age, he is still considered formidable physically. I know his tattoo span his chest boldly showing his loyalty and position in the Bratva. His dark hair has sprinkles of gray on each side now, and his bright blue eyes have lines that I don't remember being there before. He has my mother's name tattooed by his heart and still wears his wedding ring to this day. I'm sure he's not lacking in female company, but his heart will always be with my mother, Elaina. I've seen pictures of them, and even on paper, you could feel the power and love they possessed. I put a halt to these thoughts that serve no purpose in this conversation and look into my father's eyes.

"I think we have a problem in our ranks father, and with all respect to you, please listen to what I have to say before you dismiss this." I don't break eye contact.

BABA YAGA

"Okay, Anya, I will listen. Keep in mind that once an accusation is made, it can't be taken back and will be taken seriously. Are you ready for the consequences of that?"

"I am Father, I would never come to you and say such things if I thought I could be mistaken," I calmly say before telling him what I had left out of my earlier report.

I question why Kolinski was here so often and why he was getting payouts. I also wonder what dealings he was in with underage girls that caught the FBI's attention and how that led back to us. I tell him about the secret meeting Brian witnessed, Kolinski's death, Alexey and Sergei's involvement, and finish with Vlad shooting Brian in the head when I was finally getting all the information I needed. I also confess to the altercation between Vlad and me after the shooting.

"If it was one small thing, I would dismiss this, but in relaying all this information to you, I can tell that there are things you were not made aware of. Why were we paying that piece of shit? What the fuck was he doing that brought a fed to our door? Why was Vlad meeting with him? And why, right when I'm about to get a name, did Vlad shoot a man I was tasked with? All this together doesn't add up, Father. My gut has never failed me. You raised me to be ruthless, calculating, and see what others don't want me to. My instincts tell me Vlad is not loyal, and Alexey, along with Sergei, are either involved or at least know something. With your permission, I'd like to investigate this, discreetly of course."

There I've done it; I've accused my father's right-hand man along with two of our captains of disloyalty. I think I might actually be sick, the weight of my words now churning my stomach as I await his answer.

He sits, slowly rubbing his chin with his fingers, the mask I get told I so eloquently wear I inherited from him. He looks cold and calculating, mulling over all the information I've shared.

I'm starting to regret speaking up when he says, "This is what will happen, Anya. Say nothing of this conversation to anyone." As I go to interrupt, he holds up a hand. "I need you to listen to me, daughter. Not a word to Vlad, don't make him think or suspect you believe anything is amiss, same goes for Sergei and Alexey. I do want you to discreetly investigate our guest that is being disposed of but don't get caught, and you can't use any of your normal resources, am I understood?"

I nod and he continues, "Disloyalty is a death sentence for a brother, and if any plot against me is found, it's much worse. I will cut your mark from your body for all to see before you are beaten in disgrace and eventually killed."

He pauses, visibly agitated. My father has served as Pakhan since he was twenty-one and survived the coup that killed his father. You don't have the reign my father has had without getting your hands very bloody. In my lifetime, nobody has ever challenged him and succeeded.

"I understand, and you have my word. I will do as you ask, Father." I answer like the loyal soldier I am.

I stand, walk over to my father, and kneel by his chair. He cups the side of my face and slowly rubs his thumb across my cheek. These moments are rare these days, so I close my eyes to enjoy it, but the moment is robbed by a

BABA YAGA

knock at the door. Going to the door, I open it to find the man of the hour himself sporting a tank top and a nice-sized bandage covering the stitches I surely gave him.

"Looks like Victor fixed you right up, Vlad." I smile so sweetly. "If you'll both excuse me, I have somebody else's day to ruin."

I look back and nod at my father before sidestepping Vlad and heading to my office for Brian's phone, another drink, and some plans to make.

Returning to my office, I find somebody had been there. The place had been searched, and they had attempted to put it back together but failed. All my drawers had been opened, looked through, and not quite closed as if worried I might return too soon for them to finish. I walk to the large abstract painting I have hanging to the left of my desk, where my main safe is. Moving the painting aside, I see my safe has been unlocked and rifled through, leaving the cash, passports, and documents in there but not bothering to lock it back up. Something tells me the phone I took off the dead agent is what they were looking for, so I walk to my ensuite and notice my drawers and closet have been looked through as well. I go to the vanity mirror, press a button in the ornate inlay, and the mirror unlatches and swings open. I place my hand on the scanner and then enter my passcode, which releases the door to my secondary safe. Sitting right where I left it is Brian's phone. People always underestimate me, and I find it quite humorous. I'm the only person who knows I have a secondary safe in my office with better security measures. I could essentially keep everything in here, but then anyone breaking in and finding the main one

SARAH JANE

empty would, in turn, become suspicious and take a closer look elsewhere. I slip the phone into the inside pocket of my leather jacket and have just finished locking everything up when Alexey walks into my bathroom, so I pretend to be fixing my makeup.

"You know better than to walk in here without knocking, Alexey. What do you want?"

"I came to speak with you about the events earlier today and my involvement, so there is no confusion between us, Anya," he says.

"What might I be confused about, Alexey? The fact that the FBI agent saw you before I interrogated him or that you didn't make myself or my father aware before you nabbed him?" I say before walking past him and straight to my desk, where I sit down, open my laptop, and pull up the hidden surveillance cameras I have in my office. Time to find out who paid me a visit.

Alexey approaches my desk as he's talking but quickly stops to look over my shoulder and asks, "What are you doing, Anya?"

"I had an uninvited guest in my office while I was with my father. I'm just taking a little look to find out who that might've been. Better hope it wasn't you, Alexey. You're already on my shit list," I say as my feed loads up.

Every office has surveillance provided by our people for the whole building, but being who I am, I installed a more discreet system in case something like this occurred. If I were to look at security footage from the main server, I'm sure I'd find an "issue," so let's see what my cameras picked up.

Right on cue, Vlad and Sergei enter my office on the

feed. Sergei stands to watch by the door, and Vlad begins searching my office. He doesn't look happy that he can't find what he's looking for, as demonstrated by him punching the top of my desk.

I'm thoroughly amused by this, but I turn to gauge Alexey's behavior. The man never was a good actor, and he seems genuinely surprised to see these two men in my office.

"What are they doing going through your shit, and what are they looking for?"

His eyebrows pinch together, watching the two men attempt to right things and then walk out.

"Probably looking for Brian's cell phone, which I took with me as I left, and he's pissed he can't find it. Now, tell me what you've been up to, and we can fill in some holes in this situation."

I nod to the chair across from my desk, and Alexey walks around the table and takes a seat.

"My loyalty has and will always be with Anatoli Gorbachev, Anya. He has been like a father to me, and you and I have known each other since we were children. I've noticed things this last while that go against your father and the code we pledged allegiance to. Your father was aware that Brian might name me in the interrogation but felt I needed to be present regardless. And I was with Vlad when we grabbed Kolinski because I've taken a special interest in anything that seems to hold the interest of the Butcher as of late. I have made myself useful to him, and I report back to Anatoli," he says calmly and matter-of-factly.

I can tell there is no deceit in his voice.

"Thank you, Alexey, for your honesty. I never meant to

question your loyalty. However, these last few days have brought up questions I never thought I would ask. Things are not adding up. We have feds showing up here and for a lowlife piece of shit that I thought was just here to fuck our women. My intuition is never wrong, you know this. My gut tells me this is just the beginning, Alexey, and unfortunately, we're late to this party. I won't allow anything to happen to my father, and I will bring the fires of hell to anyone who gets in my way." Taking a deep breath, I lean back in my chair and stare into the bright blue eyes of my childhood friend, seeing my anger mirrored back at me.

He's quiet for a few moments, mulling over everything we have discussed. Then he says, "Well, it seems we both have the same suspicions whether we voice them or not, so moving forward, we need to be very careful. He can't know you think anything is amiss, and I can't waver in my helpful behavior. First thing, though, we need to clone that phone you have of Brian's. That way, you can continue the investigation, and I can take the phone to Vlad, thus showing my loyalty to him. We can't use the men in-house so I assume you have a way to do this?"

"I do. I'll get Liam on a plane first thing tomorrow morning back to Ireland- I still don't know where he fits into all this- and then I'll get the phone handled and text you a location and time to do a handoff. Agreed?" I stand feeling exhausted and needing this day to just end.

"I don't know what the O' Conners have to do with this. Maybe nothing at all, just bad timing, but either way, be careful, Anya. I know you care for this man, and he will always be nothing more than collateral damage." He nods and exits my office with a soft click of the door.

BABA YAGA

Nothing more can be done tonight, so I'll do my usual rounds to the security office, front desk, and casino to make sure everything is running smoothly. Then I'm taking my ass home for a long bath and glass of wine to rid myself of this day.

CHAPTER 19

LIAM

I haven't seen Anya since she left me standing in an elevator with my dick hanging out. Thank God I had the sense to tuck myself back in when the doors to the elevator opened. I had just let the doors close when Anya got out and ended up two floors down, and the woman entering the elevator looked taken aback at first seeing me shirtless, disheveled, and smelling of sex before eye fucking me down to the main floor. Her parting words for me were her room number and a time. Any other time I would've taken her up on that offer, but I'm all fucked up over a woman I was told to stay away from. I ride the elevator back up to my floor, exit, and head to my room.

I call down to the boys to let them know I'm okay and go over the itinerary for our flights home tomorrow. Home.

BABA YAGA

A place I always long for when away, and yet, I feel this time I'm leaving something behind when I go back. Fuck I'm turning into a pussy over a woman I've known for a few days. And it's more than the sex, although that is top-notch.

I spoke to my father briefly and apologize for my part in his injuries and for what I said. He wouldn't hear of it and took full responsibility for how he handled the conversation and did his best to smooth things over. I could tell he was still hiding things from me, but I didn't want to cause him any more stress, so I changed the subject and congratulated him on his new job instead. Maybe I am way off base, and this is his chance to clean up, make a new life for himself, and gain some independence for both of us.

I've packed my bags, done some yoga, and watched mindless shows on the television. My thoughts keep circling back to her, the mystery of it all, and that look on her face as she said goodbye. I'm in Vegas, the city of sin, and debauchery and I'm on the couch in a pair of sweats, watching a fucking cooking show. Decision made, I get up, stroll into my room, and change into a pair of jeans, and a T-shirt. I grab my wallet and head out the door.

I'm waiting for the elevator when it opens, and a waiter with a cart of food and a bottle of wine on ice is inside. He looks confused to see me standing there, so I back up a few steps allowing him to exit.

"Sorry, Mate, but I didn't order room service tonight," I say, thinking there must've been a mix-up.

He returns my confused look and turns the cart toward the end of the hall, where I'm just now noticing another set of double doors.

SARAH JANE

"This isn't for you, Sir. The order is for Miss Gorbachev. If you'll excuse me, this is my first day, and I'd rather not get fired." He nods and starts to push the cart down the hall.

So that's where she lives. I'm getting an idea, a very stupid idea, but my feet move me in the direction the waiter is going without a second thought. I catch up to him right as he knocks. I stay to the side so I'm not in her line of sight.

Anya opens the door, tells the man to come in, leave the cart in the living space, and leave. He proceeds in and, I assume, follows instructions as he returns a few moments later.

"Thank you, Miss Gorbachev. Have a great rest of your evening," he says and exits her room, leaving me just enough time to put my foot in the doorway before it closes.

He looks ready to sound the alarm, so I pull out $100 and hand it to him with a promise for his silence. He looks unsure until I hand him another $100. He nods and walks away with a smile, and I slip into Anya's penthouse.

Her room is not what I expected. For one, it's two floors with a staircase to my right. The rest looks like it mirrors mine, but it's more personal. This is her home, not just a place to stay while she's at work. Music filters down the stairs and water is running, so I choose to snoop before I announce myself.

I walk over to the long wall running parallel to the stairs to look at the photos lining a long cabinet. There are a few of Anya with her father, places I don't know, and in the center is a photo of a much younger Anatoli and a beautiful woman that must be Anya's mother- the resemblance is

110

uncanny. The hair color and eyes match Anya's, but that smile she gets from her father. Who knew he could smile? I stand for a moment more, intruding on her memories and trying to get closer to the mysterious woman I crave.

My dick twitches in my jeans. Now is as good a time as any to make my presence known. Kicking off my shoes and socks, I creep toward the stairs and take them two at a time, heading in the direction of the noise.

The top of the stairs opens to her bedroom, and holy motherfucking Christ, my kitten likes to play. Only someone that dabbles in BDSM would notice the rings attached to the wall, currently holding the curtains back on the canopy bed, double as hooks for cuffs or rope. Or the matching inlay on the footboard for the ankle counterparts. She's just full of surprises. I wonder what else she has hidden in here. There's sexy lingerie laying on the bed, giving me pause for a nanosecond that she's expecting somebody else, but I dismiss it and slowly walk to the ensuite. I'm transfixed as Anya pulls her hair up in some messy bun, slowly lets her robe fall to the floor, and steps into a giant standing tub. I have no words. I can't move. I just stand there as she begins to wash herself.

ANYA

Today has been a day. My mind is in overdrive; I'm feeling trapped and like a hostage in my life. Sounds a little dramatic, I know, but these past few days, I've felt things I never thought I could, such as guilt, regret, resentment, and something that resembles the L word, but I'm not saying that out loud. The logical part of my brain is wondering why the hell I'm questioning my place and the loyalty I have to the Bratva- which until now had been unwavering- for a man.

My instincts tell me Vlad is planning something to overthrow my father and claim his seat and me. Only I have no proof, just a feeling. The conversation with my father and Alexey today rattled me, but I don't do rattled. So here I am, ordering room service and climbing into my tub to wash away the day and my sins.

I throw my hair up in a messy bun, let my robe drop, and step into the tub. I settle against the back of the tub and slowly wash my arms when the hair on the back of my neck stands up. I'm not alone.

I'm planning my next move when I catch a whiff of a smell that's slowly becoming my favorite. Liam is here. I don't know how he got in here, but I suddenly feel better that he is.

I continue to slowly wash myself, adding in a few sighs and moans as my muscles relax. Might as well fuck with him if he's going to be a voyeur.

"How did you get in here, Liam?" I say without looking toward the door.

He inhales sharply, obviously surprised I knew it was him.

"If you're going to intrude and stare, at least make yourself useful. Get over here and wash my back."

BABA YAGA

I hold the loofah up and over my shoulder. It's a foregone conclusion that he'll do as I asked.

"I do like when your bossy, love, and as to how I got in here, I have my ways," he growls huskily at me as he stalks toward the tub.

He stops just before the edge, and I see a flash of fabric in my peripheral vision get tossed on the floor. He removes his shirt before falling to his knees by the tub and takes my offered loofah. He starts slow, washing my shoulders before slightly pushing so I'm leaning forward on my knees with my face resting on my arms wrapped around my legs. This man, his hands, his voice strip away the walls I worked so hard to build.

"Tell me a story, Liam. Tell me something good," I whisper and close my eyes, surrendering to the kneading of his hands and fingers.

"The smell of lavender reminds me of my mum, she loved it. Always had fresh bunches in the house. Funny the things you remember. Some days I struggle to bring her face to my mind, but I smell lavender, and it all floods back. Her smile lit up a room, and the sound of her laughter made you want to do whatever it took just to hear it again. It's the same as yours," he says quietly.

I don't want to break this moment, so I stay silent. He tells me of Ireland, of green fields for miles, his friends whom he calls family, and dreams that can never be reality. He laughs as he recalls youthful mistakes, and I can hear the smile on his face without even seeing it. I can picture it all through his words. I laugh and smile so big it hurts my face.

This feels so personal and intimate. A moment in time

113

that will haunt me forever. I've never had gentle. Being taken care of is so foreign to me, and it's intense.

I feel the loss of his hands as he gets up. After walking to the glass shower in the corner, he grabs my shampoo, conditioner, and the pitcher sitting in an antique basin just outside the shower on a wooden chair.

"What are you doing, Liam?" I ask hesitantly and look over my shoulder at him.

"I'm taking care of you tonight, Anya. Don't think, love, just be here with me. Okay?" he says as he returns to his knees behind me.

I simply nod, and he gently removes the band holding my hair up, then massages my scalp as it falls back down my shoulders. He picks up the pitcher and fills it with water before pouring it over my head, careful not to get it in my eyes, and proceeds to wash my hair. He lathers the soap into my hair, speaking words in Gaelic I don't understand.

This is the most sensual and surreal moment of my life. I feel myself yearning for this to never end. I'll daydream of nights spent talking to him just like this.

He rinses and repeats with the conditioner with such focus and care I'm overwhelmed with emotions I can't name. When he's finished, he moves around the tub so I can see him remove the rest of his clothes.

I arch my brow at him, smirking when he gives me a boyish look that I'm sure has broken hearts everywhere. Well, that thought can fuck off- no room for that right now. My eyes roam his body, starting with his eyes moving to his lips I can practically feel on mine. I lower my gaze to his chest, covered in beautiful ink, down to his abs I want to lick, and to his thick cock, already hard and at attention.

BABA YAGA

He gives it a leisurely stroke causing me to lick my bottom lip and bite down. My nipples pebble, and my pussy throbs as he steps into the tub with me and sits

down facing me. He lifts my left foot from the water, placing it on his midsection. With firm hands, he begins to massage my foot. The last of my stress slowly seeps from my body.

I can't help the moan that slips from my lips as I close my eyes and tilt my head back against the tub. I've died and gone to heaven. I must have. Nothing else can explain this. My body is on fire, and I don't know where I need attention most. I'm moaning and squirming, yet he keeps a firm grip, kneading and rubbing all my stress away.

He finishes the left foot, returning it to the water, grabs my right, and repeats the same treatment. My breath is coming in short bursts. I need him more than air.

"Please, Liam. Mmm mm. Please touch me. I need you," I plead with him.

"Touch yourself, Anya. Show me where you're needy, love," he says huskily as he continues the sensual onslaught on my feet.

I obey his command without thought, lifting my hands to caress my breasts. I knead them in each hand, working toward my nipples that ache. I pinch and roll them, arching my back and thrashing my head. The slight sting of the pinch and the soft rolling between my fingers is so bitter-sweet. I feel the orgasm building inside me. I let one hand slowly trail down my stomach toward my clit while the other keeps up the delicious rhythm on each breast. My fingers find my button and begin slow circles, which become faster and more frantic as I chase the orgasm I couldn't stop even if I wanted to. At some point, Liam stopped rubbing my foot. I'm so close, it's right there.

"Oh god. Fuck yes, Liiaaaammmmm!"

I come hard, riding the waves. When the fog clears, I open my eyes to look at Liam, trying to slow my breathing down. The raw, unadulterated look of hunger I see in his eyes has my breath quickening again.

He leans forward, places his hands on my waist, and pulls me toward him, sloshing water all over the floor. I squeal a little but swallow it down as he pulls me onto his lap, spreading my legs to rest on either side of his. I can feel his rock-hard cock rub against my pussy.

"Come here, baby," he says as he uses both hands to pull my arms behind my back.

He keeps one hand holding both wrists in a firm grip and fists the other into my hair. He pulls my head back, arching my back enough for his mouth to latch onto a breast and mercilessly suck. The pain is delicious, causing me to scream out and move my hips enough for some friction on his cock. I'll have marks tomorrow from his hunger as he sucks and nibbles each breast and then travels up my neck, licking and marking me as his, all while I rock myself on his dick.

Using my hair to tilt my head, he takes my mouth, fucking my mouth with his tongue, pillaging and taking his due. Leveraging the hand holding my wrists against my spine, he pulls me forward and up just enough to place his thick head at my entrance. Then he drags me down his length till I'm fully seated. We break contact, groaning with pleasure.

BABA YAGA

He rests his forehead against my chest, inhales, and whispers,

"Fuck, Anya, your pussy feels so good wrapped around my cock, choking it. I'm going to release you now, so be a good girl and ride my cock."

He releases my hair and wrists and leans back, wrapping his arms around the sides of the tub.

I'll be a good girl, all right. Starting slow, I swivel my hips in a lazy circle going clockwise, then counterclockwise. He grunts, giving me the look of a starving man, and grabs my ass with a bruising grip.

"I said fucking ride my cock, baby."

My restraint snaps. Fuck gentle, then. I pick up speed, rubbing my clit on the base of his cock. There is no finesse to my movements, it's just primal lust pushing me to ecstasy

"God, your cock feels so good, so full. I want that cum. I'm so close, Liam. Fill me up, fill me up, yes, yes, yes!" I'm chanting as I feel myself tip over the edge and explode.

At this point, I think more water is on the floor than in the tub, but I don't give a shit. I want this man at my mercy, not in control, and spiraling as much as I am. His breathing is getting quicker, dirty words fall from his mouth.

"That's a good girl. My turn. Take it, Anya. Milk my cock, here it comes, fuck," he bellows and thrusts up, emptying himself.

I keep moving, wringing every last drop from him, and we collapse.

I can't move, but my legs are aching, and it's starting to get cold with no water left in the tub, so I attempt to pull back. Liam moves quickly to wrap his arms around me, keeping us connected.

"I got you, Love, hold on," he says before wrapping one arm under my ass and using the other against the tub to push himself up and to his feet.

I quickly wrap my arms around his neck and hook my legs around his waist, so I don't fall. I've never been manhandled before, and I have to say I'm not opposed to it. He steps out of the tub and slowly walks toward the bedroom, trying not to slip on the soaking-wet floor. I can't help the laughter that falls from my lips as he stops at the end of the bed and tosses me, sending me flat on my back after a bounce or two.

Lust and hunger is written all over his face when he gives me that sexy smirk and grabs both ankles, spreading my legs wide. Starting at one ankle, he kisses, licks, and nibbles his way up to my center. He licks me from back to front, then pulls back and gives the same attention to my other leg, starting at my ankle and moving back up to my pussy.

I feel like a starved woman. I can't get enough of this man as he licks me again, I reach down, gripping his head, not allowing him to move.

"Like that?" He chuckles before blowing air on my already engorged clit before diving back in and flicking his tongue.

Holy fuck, this man will be the death of me.

LIAM

Baba Yaga

I could eat her out all night long with no arguments. This woman completely undoes me. I have no rational thoughts when I'm in her arms, and what just happened in the bathroom is imprinted into my soul for the rest of time. I sound like a complete pussy, but I don't care.

She tugs my hair, which is just long enough for her to grab hold of. It seems my thoughts have distracted me away from giving my woman- yes, I said my woman- another orgasm. Flicking my tongue back and forth on her clit I slide two fingers into her tight wet hole and curl them just enough to hit her sweet spot. Then I fuck her hard. The sounds she's making have my dick so hard that the slightest friction or touch will have me coming like a teenage boy, but I'm not stopping till she coats my chin in her cum.

"Liam, fuck yes, faster, harder, right there." She moans as her pretty pussy clamps down on my fingers, and then she screams my name.

I don't stop licking and sucking till my chin is dripping, and she tries to push my head away.

"Too much, so sensitive," she mumbles.

"I'm not done with you yet, love," I tell her as I lick my lips. "You taste like heaven, and I want more," I add while I kiss my way up her body, stopping just long enough to suck and nibble each of her beautiful tits before capturing her lips and burying my cock in her pussy.

She wraps her legs around my waist, digs her heels in, and wraps her arms around my neck as we kiss. For the first time in my life, I make love to a woman. I caress her everywhere I can reach with my hands and lips, thrusting with long strokes so I feel every inch of her as she does me. When I feel her clamp down, I lift my head, and we look into each other's eyes as we both explode. No words are spoken as we come down.

I gently pull out, grab a washcloth from the bathroom, wet it, and come back to clean up her. Once finished, I discard the cloth and climb under the covers wrapping Anya up in my arms. I watch her face as she smiles contentedly, laying her head on my chest. With the food and wine long forgotten downstairs, I pull the covers back up over us. Her face is the last thing I see before I drift off to sleep.

CHAPTER 20

ANYA

I don't think I've ever slept so soundly in my life as I did wrapped up in Liam's arms last night. I should evaluate that, but I need to pee. I open my eyes and stare at him for a moment, watching him breathe with one arm flopped across his forehead and the other still circled around me. I wriggle to get out from under his arm and make my way to the bathroom. I'm washing my hands when I hear a phone go off. Looking down, I see the light from Liam's phone sticking out from his jeans. I pick it up to see ten missed calls and half a dozen messages. I hate to disturb Liam, but this must be important, so I go back into the bedroom and, lean over to place a kiss on his lips.

"Time to get up, Handsome. Your phone is going crazy," I say as he slowly comes to, giving me that pantry-

SARAH JANE

dropping grin that's growing on me more and more every day.

I hand him his phone, and his eyebrows shoot up when he sees the screen. I figure I'll give him some privacy to get up and deal with whatever is going on, so I head downstairs to the fridge to see if there's anything to eat. I skipped dinner for dick last night, and I'm starving. Won't hear me complaining, though.

I grab my phone off the docking station as I walk past and open a cupboard to grab a glass. It slips from my fingers, shattering on the floor, as I swipe to see I have several missed calls and messages as well. I click on the first message just as I hear Liam bang against the wall.

"Fuck, shit damn," he's hollering as he comes into view, hurriedly pulling clothes on. "Anya! Check your phone, love."

I look down and read message after message, getting more irate, asking me where Liam is, where I am, and why I'm not answering. The last one from Vlad states he's on his way to my place, and I better be alone.

Fuck is right. I look up at Liam, and it all clicks. He's supposed to be on a plane back to Ireland- I glance at the clock- in less than two hours, and we were supposed to be at breakfast with my father before he left. I fly past Liam and yell orders over my shoulder as I go.

"Liam, get the fuck back to your place and grab your shit. We have to go. Be quick, Vlad is on his way here, and you better not be here when he arrives."

I hate being so harsh, but I was warned, and I disregarded the order to stay away from him. I was selfish and wanted something for myself, and it might cost us both.

122

BABA YAGA

I'm halfway up the stairs when I hear the door open, when Liam yells, "Anya, love, you better come back here."

My blood runs cold.

I slowly come back down to find Liam at the door, shoes in one hand, holding the door open with the other. Vlad stands on the other side, ready to commit murder by the look he's giving Liam. His eyes look past Liam and meet mine. The world drops out from under my feet. I'm going to pay for this.

Vlad pushes past Liam and walks to meet me at the bottom of the stairs. Looking into his eyes, void of any soul, I bolster my strength. I will not show this man fear.

"Go put some clothes on, Anya. Now. Your father wishes to see you now. Alexey will be escorting Liam to the airport in your place." He looks back at Liam, pulls his lip back in a snarl, and says, "Run along little man. Alexey is waiting outside your room. It's time you fuck off back to your own country. I'd say it's been a pleasure, but I'd be lying."

Liam looks over at me, seemingly torn between leaving and wanting to throat-punch Vlad. I give a subtle shake of my head which earns me a grunt and a wink before he walks out the door.

"You must have a magic pussy Anya for him to obey so easily. I won't be so easily swayed," Vlad says with such venom you'd almost think it was jealousy, but that would require this man to have a soul.

I give him my back, heading up the stairs to get dressed. Better not leave my father waiting; this meeting won't go well.

Walking into my bedroom, I glance at the rumpled bed,

and a ghost of a smile crosses my face. Standing in my closet, I feel the scrutiny of Vlad's stare behind me. There's no point telling him to leave, angering him further won't help me. I slip on a thong and a pair of black leggings before dropping my robe, putting on a black sports bra, and finishing with a light off-shoulder T-shirt. Might as well be comfortable for the shit show.

Walking past Vlad, I go into my bathroom and almost slip on the still-wet floor, causing me to laugh at how much of a mess we made last night. Tiptoeing to the sink, I quickly brush my teeth, run a brush through my tousled hair, and pull it back into a ponytail. I see the Butcher in the reflection of my mirror as he takes in the scene in front of him. When our eyes meet, he's seething with hatred and malice. I'm terrified of this man, but I refuse to resign my life to him without experiencing joy at least once.

I do not doubt in my mind that Vlad will be the death of me after he uses me all up in his perverted violent ways. I'll be disposable. He wants my father's seat and an heir. Once I give him those things through marriage, and most likely rape because I won't give him my body willingly, I will no longer be useful and, therefore, a liability. These thoughts will not taint this space. I won't allow it. So, it's time to get the mask in place and go see the Pakhan for my punishment.

We exit my suite and find Liam and Alexey waiting at the elevator. Both men look me over, making sure I have no sign of injury. Liam looks ready to fight a war for me, and Alexey gives me a sincere brotherly look of concern before looking at Vlad and nodding.

We enter the elevator together and ride down to the next

floor when the doors open to allow Mac, Finn, Patty, Ronan, and Declan onto the elevator. Declan still looks a little worse for wear but wants to see his son off safely. Each man makes eye contact with me, nods, and faces forward. Only Ronan and Declan's eyes linger. Ronan looks suspicious and concerned while Declan looks afraid. His bad choices will catch up to him soon, and I will do everything I can to make sure his son doesn't pay for his mistakes. Liam slips in between Alexey and Finn to stand beside me. He grabs my hand and gives me the slightest squeeze. I'm selfish, so I soak in all the strength he gives me in such a simple way. Nobody disobeys Anatoli, and I did it in spades. Being his daughter won't protect me from his anger.

The elevator reaches the main floor, and everyone files out. They pause, waiting for Liam and me to follow. This isn't the goodbye I wanted but knowing I'll see him in a few short weeks when he's back for the title fight gives me peace.

"Have a safe flight back, gentlemen. It has been a pleasure, and I hope to see you all when Liam returns for his chance at the title." I muster out the words and receive kind words from them in return.

I don't want to look at Liam, so I quickly say goodbye and turn to walk away.

"Not so fast, Love. That's not how we're saying goodbye," Liam says, grabbing my wrist and pulling me in to kiss me with every bit of passion he gave last night.

I get lost for a moment in his arms before I'm yanked from him by Vlad.

"You need to learn your place motherfucker, and one

day soon, I will take great pleasure in teaching you," Vlad spits in Liam's direction, as he attempts to pull me away.

"We shall see, big man. Now run along like the good little lap dog you are."

This situation is getting out of hand, and we are drawing too much attention standing in the damn lobby. I pull my arm free of the Butcher's grip and do what I should've done before it got this far.

"That's enough, Liam. The sex was great, but let's be honest, this had an expiration date. This was business, and now it's time to go."

My world is falling apart as I realize I do have a heart, and it's breaking. I take a good, long, hard look at Liam so I can memorize everything before I mouth the words good-bye. Liam looks poised for a fight with all his friends beside him. I envy that kind of loyalty.

"That's enough. We don't have time for a pissing contest. Liam, time to go, son. You'll miss your flight," Declan interjects trying to defuse the situation, which seems to work as everyone, except Liam turns, picks up their bags, and proceeds to the entrance.

Liam picks up his bag and hesitates for a moment, torn about how to proceed.

He looks at me with a sad smile and says, "MO GHRÀ THU, MO STÒR." *(You are my love, my treasure.)*

Then he turns and walks away, passing his friends, who look shocked by whatever he just said.

I don't have enough time to figure out what just happened because I'm once again pulled by the arm toward the hallway leading to my father's office. I'm struggling to free my arm from Vlad's iron grip, but he's not letting me go this time. He stops outside my father's office and knocks, showing at least some respect for who is actually in charge here.

We hear "come in" from the other side, so Vlad opens the door, shoving me inside and causing me to almost lose my balance. Wouldn't help to fall on my ass when I need to be strong, facing what I know will be a painful lesson in obedience. I regain my balance, stand tall, and pull my shoulders back. My father isn't alone. Standing behind him on either side are Sergei and Dmitry. This is worse than I thought.

"Come here, Daughter."

I approach his desk and attempt to take a seat.

"Don't bother sitting, Anya." He flicks his fingers in a gesture toward Sergei and Dmitry, who come around his desk, picks the two chairs up, and move them away before taking up a place on either side of me.

"I gave you express orders to stay away from that fighter, Anya. Orders I expected to be followed. I should turn you over to Alexey for the whore house if you are going to choose to act like a bitch in heat, but I need the skills you possess, so I'm left with a decision to make. The Butcher was kind enough to make some suggestions. I will not be disobeyed, daughter or not, you will know the consequences of defying me. Do we understand each other?" he says so calmly, but I feel the full force of his anger.

"I understand, Father, and I accept any punishment you see fit," I manage to say

I see Vlad removing his suit jacket and rolling up the sleeves on his bright white dress shirt, slowly walking toward the desk.

SARAH JANE

"I don't want a single mark on her face Butcher or anywhere visible. Understand? Now begin," my father says.

Sergei and Dmitry grab my arms to hold me upright as Vlad lands the first punch to my gut, knocking the air from my lungs. Trying to suck in as much air as I can, I prepare for the next hit, which comes hard and fast to the ribs on my right side. Gulping and wheezing, I'm too slow to see the blow to my left side before it lands. Judging by the spots in front of my eyes and the dizziness, I suspect a few ribs are either cracked or broken. Vlad continues to rain blows to each side; I'm starting to slump forward, but the goons just pull me upright again so he can keep going.

He gets another few blows in before I hear my father say, "that's enough," and he backs up. I notice blood on his knuckles from punching me with those gaudy ass rings he wears. He must've broken skin, but I won't give that bastard the satisfaction of looking now. So, in true Anya fashion, I raise my head and give him my best smile.

"You hit like a girl." And I spit in his face.

Wrong move. Rage distorts his features as he steps forward and slaps me across the face so hard that, I think my head might fly off my shoulders. Sergei and Dmitry let me go allowing me to fall to my knees as they go to hold back Vlad.

My father gets up, walking slowly around his desk until he's standing in front of Vlad. The Butcher is taller and wider than my father, but each wields power in their own way. I sometimes wonder who is the lesser evil. Anatoli reaches for Sergei's sheathed knife at his side and withdraws it. He inspects it, feeling its weight before lifting it so it's within Vlad's eyesight. My lip's bleeding down my chin while I try to catch my breath, yet I won't move a muscle until granted permission.

"I see lessons must be handed out to more than my daughter today, Butcher. I said don't touch her face." With that, he grabs a chunk of Vlad's hair, pulls his head back, and slowly cuts a line from his left eye to his jawline. He then wipes the blade on Vlad's shirt and returns the blade to the sheath he took it from.

"You are dismissed. Get the fuck out of my office."

Vlad is released. He grabs his jacket from the chair he discarded it on and storms from the room. The other two nod at my father and exit, promptly shutting the door quietly.

Anatoli turns to face me, looking at the damage the Butcher has caused. He looks like he aged ten years in this moment, yet I can't muster a fuck to give.

"I sure hope you have learned your lesson, Anya. Go get checked out," he says, wiping a hand down his face. "Was he worth it?"

I slowly stand, holding my side while trying not to wobble and fall back down. Gathering the last of my strength, I look my father in the eyes and wipe my mouth. "To answer you, yes, he was worth it, but also, probably not."

His lip twitches with a hint of a smile, and I slowly shuffle to the door.

Taking one last look at my father looking at the picture of my mother on his desk, I make my exit. *Heavy is the head that wears, the crown, or however the saying goes.* I lean against the wall, putting one foot in front of the other.

SARAH JANE

My vision is blurring, and my steps are faltering. I'm not going to make it. My legs begin to give out.

"Jesus Christ, Anya, wake up. I'm here. What the fuck happened?"

Two voices talk over each other before someone's hands are on me. I recoil, trying to defend myself, and open my eyes to see who has hands on me. Alexey and Liam's father kneel beside me.

"Alexey, help me up, and Declan, this is the price I paid for falling in love with your son."

Wait, did I just say that out loud? I must be losing it. Rather than helping me up, Alexey gently lifts me into his arms, avoiding the side I'm holding onto. I'm bleeding on him, but I lose consciousness before I can feel bad about it.

"Two broken ribs on the left side, one more cracked, and several bruised on the right. Her spleen is bruised as well, and I've taken care of the gashes caused by, I'm assuming, jewelry on both sides. None required stitches, but I did glue them to be safe. She will be in pain for a few weeks. I can give her something to help with that, but none of her usual extracurriculars, Alexey. She needs rest, and keep her the fuck away from the Butcher. I sewed up his face shortly before you brought me her. He was furious. Her name passed his lips a few times." Doc's voice cuts through the fog.

I groan, alerting everyone in the room I'm coming to.

I'm lying in a bed in the "medical wing" we have set up in the back of the resort for all those emergencies we can't call attention to. It's state of the art with everything the Doc needs, including a suite for surgeries should we need it. My shirt is gone leaving me in only my sports bra and leggings.

BABA YAGA

A bandage is wrapped firmly around my midsection. Everything hurts, including my heart. With every blow Vlad landed today, part of me cracked in two. I felt stripped away like a snake shedding its skin, leaving something hollow and used. My whole life has been Bratva, following my father's orders, and this is where it has gotten me.

A hand lands gently on my shoulder, and I hear Declan whisper, "Rest, sweet girl, you've earned it. I'm sorry this happened to you." He gives me a slight squeeze.

"Declan don't go yet. I need to ask you a question. What did Liam say to me before he left today?" I pause. "Please," I manage, already feeling tired. Doc must've given me the good stuff.

"I thought you might ask; it won't help either of you knowing, but looking at you now, I won't deny your request. He said 'you are my love, my treasure.' His eyes fill with tears. "I said the same to his mother when I knew she was it for me." Wiping his eyes, he looks at me with such sadness and walks away.

I want to say something, give comfort, but the drugs kicking in. Alexey grabs my hand and tells me he'll watch over me, so I surrender to the darkness.

CHAPTER 21

ANYA

Alexey kept his word that day and never left my side. When Doc cleared him to take me, he placed me in a wheelchair and took me home. We had a silent agreement never to talk about my confessions, or Declan's for that matter, but I felt a shift in our relationship.

Recovery was slow and frustrating. The first week, I barely saw a soul, and all traces of my sexcapades were erased from my home, leaving it feeling cold once more. Doc made regular visits to check that I wasn't overexerting myself, and Alexey checked in several times a day to bring food. He even watched movies with me at night, reminding me of times when we were children. My father was absent, only sending notes and messages through Alexey. And Vlad sported a scar for his ignorance. Small

BABA YAGA

victories, I guess. Now the ugly on the inside matches the outside.

On the seventh day after my lesson, I ordered Alexey to bring me my laptop so I could at least keep up with emails and other duties. I may have threatened him with violence, to which he chuckled. I politely reminded him I would recover, and that I have a long memory. My laptop arrived within the hour. I'm glad somebody is still afraid of me. I thought I was losing my touch.

I open my emails to find a long list of things I've left unattended, so I start at the bottom and work my way back up to the most recent. Orders are filled, and I go over payroll, double-checking everything balances. I note payment was made to a contractor, although nothing is mentioned about who or what services were rendered, just a number and account info. I open a file and make notes of anything irregular I find. After an hour or so, I order food. Looking back at my notes, I see a pattern of "contractors" being paid, all with different numbers assigned but all going to the same bank account. I add it to the list of things I'm looking into when Victor gives me the all-clear to get back to my life.

Let's be honest I haven't been a model patient. Between my line of work and knowing intimately what Vlad's fists feel like- and believe me, I know he held back- I will not be weak, so I've been moving more than I should, doing light stretches, and squats because I'm a glutton for punishment, and throwing knives at targets I move around my room.

Speaking of stretching thoughts of Liam pop into my mind as I loosen up. That first day when I walked in to find him doing yoga, all that skin, and ink, the way his body moved so effortlessly. I was captivated by him, and I still am. He's never been far from my thoughts since he left. I don't know what the coming weeks will bring. I know daydreaming about a future we can't have won't help me. I just wish I could be worthy of his love. A soul as black as mine with a trail of bodies doesn't deserve to be called anyone's treasure despite how much I yearn for it.

Shaking free from my wayward thoughts, I'm almost through the emails when I come across one from a sender I don't recognize. I open it to find a brief message from Ronan telling me he still thinks I'm trouble, which makes me chuckle because he's not wrong, and that "our boy"- I do like the sound of that- is in the thick of training for the fight with a determination Ronan has never seen before, which he hates to admit might have something to do with me. A video is attached to the email, and when I open it, Liam must be in Danver's gym. I can't help but smile as he runs through drills, shadowboxes, and grapples with Mac and Finn in the cage. Ronan and his father- I'm assuming that's who it is based on looks and the pride on his face- are barking orders at Liam on placement and protecting his blindside. The video cuts to them watching reels of the fighter he'll be facing as they dissect his style, and movements, looking for weaknesses. Liam is so focused I don't think he realizes someone is filming him until he gets a nudge from Patty and a head nod toward whoever is holding the camera. When his eyes meet the screen, I suck in my breath.

"Anything you want to say to the little lady?" That panty-dropping smile graces his face,

BABA YAGA

"I'll see you soon, love." He winks before getting back to work.

How did he know I didn't mean the words I said? He must have sensed the regret that overwhelmed me the moment they left my mouth.

I exit from the video feeling lighter and stronger. It's time for me to get back to work as well. I move slowly but with purpose as I brush my teeth, comb my hair, and pull it back into a ponytail. I throw on a sports bra, leggings, and a light T-shirt making my way downstairs.

Alexey knocks on the door and enters with the room service I had ordered.

"You shouldn't be up and about like you are, Anya. You need to rest and heal," Alexey says like he's already tired of this argument.

Waving my hand at him, I sit at my table wincing from the position, and dig into my meal. He sits across from me with the ghost of a smile as I eat like it's my last meal. He's got news or messages for me, so I give him a quick hand signal to continue as I finish eating before taking a pill to manage my pain for a few hours.

"First, your father wishes you well. He's been getting daily reports on your well-being from Viktor. Not my place to say, but I do think he feels some guilt over the events."

That earns him a small grunt from me.

"Second, I did as we discussed and turned over the phone to Vlad. He was as happy with me, as you'd thought he'd be, and almost relieved. He asked where I'd gotten it, and I fed him the lie we had agreed upon. He thinks you have a fake, and my loyalty to him is favorable now. I've been made aware he has been asking questions about you as well and was quite displeased that Viktor refused to offer anything up, claiming patient confidentiality. Thought that would make you smile just a bit, I know how happy pissing him off makes you." He chuckles just a little.

I'd share the laugh with him, but it hurts too much, so I just smile like the cat that ate the canary.

"You're right, I do love when he's miserable, but back to the business at hand. We need to move on to the next phase of my plan. I need to get out of here undetected and down to The Kitty House to speak to my girl about cracking this phone, and we need to bug Vlad's office."

Alexey shakes his head before I can even finish.

"Getting you down to the whore house will be doable, but it won't be easy. However, bugging Vlad will be a no-go. He must be paranoid, because he has his office, person, and home swept daily for bugs. He claims security purposes. I looked into it."

That bastard isn't stupid, I'll give him that, but that does set us back. I need to know who he's talking to, but first, we need to know what Brian meant to tell me before Vlad shot him.

We talk for another hour or two, coming up with a plan to get me out of here for a while. It'll involve asking Sasha to come "visit," and I'll masquerade as her to go back to The Kitty House. That gets me in easily enough but getting back still needs work. Alexey isn't fully on board with this but does agree Vlad cannot see me entering or leaving the whore house. It'll raise questions because I've never entered that establishment, my friends have always met me outside of their work to enjoy much-needed girl time. They know who I am, all my darkness, and still accept me anyway.

Alexey leaves to make the arrangements, and I practice walking back and forth in my living room to make sure I can appear normal, sexy, and uninjured for my little adventure. This plan is risky, dangerous, and a little stupid, but I know my instincts are right. I need proof for this to work, it has to.

CHAPTER 22

LIAM

It seems like forever ago since I left Vegas, and though I'm happy to be home and back at it in the gym, I feel like I left a piece of myself behind. I always thought my dad was blowing smoke up my ass about how soon and how sure he was that my mum was it for him. He said there was no point fighting it, he was a goner, and I should be so lucky to find that one day. Who knew it would be in the shape of a Russian vixen with more secrets than the Vatican? He was right, though, I'm addicted and need her like my next breath.

These next six weeks will be torture, so I pour everything into my training. This fight is my golden ticket. I want that belt badly. Danvers and the boys have me eating, sleeping, and breathing the program they developed based on my opponent to make sure I'm in the best shape and mindset to go into this prepared and ready to win.

I don't know how Ronan got Anya's email but sending her these clips of how hard I'm working and having her reply with support and tips, which I'll examine later, has made me focus that much more. I feel like everything is coming together in my career and my life. It's all I've wanted. I never realized how much more it would mean to have someone to share it with. I sound like a woman, for fuck's sake.

On that note, someone calls my name, so I hit send on the email to my woman and head back into the gym with a shit-eating grin on my face and focus like I've never had before.

ANYA

Sitting here smiling to myself after reading an email from Liam, I'm daydreaming so I don't hear the door or Alexey and Sasha enter until Alexey yells my name. I'm losing myself over this man. Giving my head a shake, I look up to meet two concerned sets of eyes looking at me.

"I'm fine. Don't worry. Just lost in my thoughts" I rise and walk over to hug my friend. "Thank you, Sasha, for coming and agreeing to help me." I slowly release her and finally get a good look at her face.

Bruises are in different stages of healing, but the scarring is minimal, thanks to the surgeon. I feel myself getting angry all over again and wishing Kolinski was alive just so I could cut his dick off and watch him bleed out again. I worry about the darkness in my soul sometimes, the depravity of the things I've done because of following orders and living a life I don't choose.

Sasha and I can at least relate to that. She grew up in Bratva as well; however, her father was involved in the coup that killed my grandfather, and the penance paid was his daughters. Sasha sold her body and soul in return for her sister's freedom. She supports them while they go to school out west and protects them with strength very few would understand. She's beautiful, kind, honest, powerful, and, besides Alexey, the closest thing to family I have. There is nothing she could ask of me that I would not do.

"Of course, little doll. I would do anything for you. Now let's get you prepped. I have clients this evening, so no fucking around or you'll be on your back earning my keep." She laughs at her joke, knowing full well it would never happen.

She sets her bag on the counter, pulls out the wig and makeup I'll need, and gets to work. Alexey sits down on the couch across the room and scrolls through his phone.

An hour goes by, and after she's transformed me, we head to my room to switch clothes. We're about the same size, except her tits were bought and paid for while mine were God-given, nothing a good push-up bra won't solve. Alexey looks up as we come down the stairs and does a double take.

"Sasha, you have outdone yourself. At this distance you

BABA YAGA

can't tell the two of you apart," he says as he stands and walks toward us.

Never able to take a compliment well, Sasha merely nods and takes Alexey's spot on my couch, grabbing a book off my side table.

"Good luck," she says and opens the book to read.

That's our cue.

We ride the elevator in silence. When we step off into the lobby area, I keep my head down, so the cameras don't get a good look at my face. We veer left past the front desk and make our way to the courtyard that houses our gardens, cafes, nightclubs, and The Kitty House. Prostitution is illegal, so The Kitty House masquerades as a strip club with unique performances in front of and behind the curtains, a selection of fantasies available for the right price.

So far so good Nobody pays us any attention. A few looks here and there, but we make it to The Kitty House, only to find Katarina indisposed with a portly old gentleman, rutting like a pig on top of her. He hasn't spotted us yet, Kat has, and she winks before holding up three fingers, counting down to zero before the Piggly wiggly finishes in what looks like a painful orgasm, sounding like he's dying.

He gets up and pulls his tan khaki pants and white stained briefs up before mumbling his thanks. As he turns to leave, he finally notices us standing by the door. The poor guy really exerted himself there. He's sweating buckets and doesn't make eye contact while hurrying from the room like his ass is on fire.

Katarina stretches out like a cat before gracefully sliding from her bed to use the bathroom quickly. I hear the

SARAH JANE

taps turn on for a moment or two then, the toilet flushes. Alexey seems to be looking anywhere but the bed and Kat as she flounces back into the room, grabbing a robe to cover up her body. Interesting.

"I'll leave you ladies to chat while I go check on the girls and make some calls," Alexey says over his shoulder as he walks from the room and shuts the door behind him.

I turn back to Kat, looking at the door with a longing I'm becoming very familiar with. Very interesting. She sees me looking and shakes her head before giving me a quick embrace.

Katarina is another woman stuck by circumstance. Beautiful, tall, graceful like a ballerina, with red hair, freckles, and a brain world leaders would fight for. After several unsavory syndicates tried to buy or coerce her, Alexey found her and gave her an out. We changed her name and brought her to America where her bright red hair and porcelain looks would be more common. To repay her debt, she offered to work on her back. Looks like both parties regret that decision. That's a problem for another day.

"I'm sorry to be involving you in this mess, but I need answers discreetly."

We let go, and I follow her to her makeup vanity.

"I know you wouldn't be asking unless this was important, but I won't risk my life by leaving a fingerprint behind, Anya," she says firmly.

Anyone worth their weight in gold among computer hackers has a specific fingerprint, as you call it, which is why until now, I had avoided asking anything of her and her hidden talents. Only Alexey and I know who she really

BABA YAGA

is. I won't risk her safety either, so I pull out the cell phone from our dead fed and hand it to her.

"I understand, and I would never let any harm come to you. I need anything you can get me off this phone. Will you be compromised?" I hold my breath, hoping I don't have to go to less savory individuals.

She takes it from me, turns back to her vanity, and pulls out a compartment under the vanity that houses her laptop. Bloody genius. She then boots it up and plugs in the phone.

"It'll take a few seconds for me to crack it. A quick in and out. As long as this phone doesn't have a tracker in place, we should be good," she says as she starts tapping on keys.

I am in awe of her skills. Her precision is an art. Seeing it firsthand, I now understand the weight of my responsibility to protect her. She clicks a few more times, and poof, everything in Brian's phone is open for me to see.

"Have I told you lately you're a fucking genius?" I say before leaning over to get a closer look at everything.

A lot of surveillance photos of Kolinski during his last visit, a quick shot of Kolinski going into the office with Vlad and Sergei, then picking up again outside The Kitty House with Vlad and Alexey leading out a bloody Kolinski. So far, the photos prove everything Brian said. Katarina looks a little concerned that Alexey is in several photos towards the end.

"Okay, so he didn't lie about why he was here. Now I need to know who he was reporting to. Can you access his phone and texts and see if any numbers show up frequently?"

"No problem, just a sec." She types a few more keys, and a list of messages and outgoing calls comes up on the screen. "Looks like your guy was calling a New York number regularly. Let me see if I can find out who that number belongs to."

A few more keystrokes and her eyebrows knit together, and then she quickly scribbles down the number before deleting everything, leaving no trace.

"What happened?" I say as she hands me the paper

"I told you, I won't risk my safety, and whoever did the work on the phone number we found is almost as good as me. It's a burner, but anyone trying to tamper and look more closely will be backtracked. Whatever you've gotten yourself into, Anya, please be careful. I can't tell you what to do but think it through before calling that number. Make sure you want to know who is on the other end."

Kat hands me the number, hides her laptop under the vanity, then leans over, touching up her makeup in the mirror.

A knock at the door indicates Kat's next client is here, so I tuck the number into my bra and walk to the door. Before I leave, I turn, taking one last look at my friend.

"Thank you, Kat. I will take your warning into consideration before moving forward. Have some faith. I am Baba Yaga, after all. I should be feared," I say, trying to break up the tension in the moment.

Before the door closes, she whispers, "There are bigger monsters in this world, Anya."

I walk away feeling off-kilter and my confidence wavering.

Meeting Alexey in his office, I nod, letting him know I

got what we needed, and we head out the side entrance to make our way back to my penthouse before anyone notices Sasha has been MIA. I'm on edge as I go over the pros and cons of calling this phone number to see who picks up. It's reckless, risky, and a little stupid, but if I'm being honest, besides with Liam, I haven't felt this exhilarated and alive in a long time. I've been stuck, concerned with how cold I was becoming. I need to know the answers. I need to prove to myself and my father that I'm more than just a killing machine, that my gut was right.

I'm just stepping onto the elevator when the Butcher comes around the corner and calls Alexey's name. Shit. That motherfucker will know it's me right away. Alexey meets my eyes before he hits the close button and steps out, giving Vlad only a glance at my long blond hair before I'm out of sight.

I release the breath I didn't realize I was holding and sink against the wall. The pain medication is wearing off, my body is screaming, and my nerves are frazzled. That was too close, and I am in no shape to go for another round with Vlad just yet.

I walk into my suite, and Sasha is curled up in the same spot, reading the book she picked up when she arrived. I don't want to catch her off guard after her ordeal, so I toss my keys into the bowl near my entrance a little harder than necessary to alert her I'm here before I speak.

"You're back. That was quicker than I thought you'd be. I don't need to know, but I do hope you got what you needed," Sasha says without taking her eyes off the page.

Note to self, actually read the books on my table.

"I did, thank you. I'd love to chat however the Butcher

caught up with Alexey and me at the elevators. He didn't see my face, but he will assume it's you and will be asking questions if you don't surface soon," I say while pulling the wig from my head and removing her clothes.

"Shit, I agree. The sooner I leave, the less likely he'll feel the need to come and check. Besides, the Butcher is on my schedule tonight, and I can only handle so much. His tastes run differently from most men's. He's violent and cruel when he fucks. Pissing him off won't help me." She lets out a long sigh and stands "Can I borrow this book?"

"Of course," I say as we quickly exchange clothes.

I don't want to think of my friend enduring Vlad in any sense. But while sex is on my mind, I think I'll keep the wig. *Maybe Liam will want to play,* I think to myself and smile. We hug at the door, and she's gone in a blink.

With nobody around to witness, I can finally remove the mask I'm forced to wear and allow my feelings to show. I grasp the banister leading upstairs, using it to help me balance. I slowly make my way to my room. My breaths are heavy, and my energy is fading. I shuffle to the bathroom, wash the makeup from my face, and take pills to help combat this pain forcing its way through my body. Slowly stripping down to my shirt and thong, I climb into bed, falling into a deep sleep.

I come to with a start a few hours later. Needing a moment to adjust, I feel around for the button on my lamp beside the bed. Soft light fills the room. It's night, but I'm starving, so I gently swing my legs over the side of the bed, hobble to the bathroom to splash water on my face, take more pain meds, and head downstairs to find something to eat.

BABA YAGA

Thirty minutes later, I've eaten and pulled out my laptop to Google the time difference in New York. They're three hours ahead of me. It's 11:00 p.m. here, so 2:00 a.m. there. Not bad. And yet I'm at my table, staring at the phone number and my cell phone hesitating. Fuck's sake. I'm the last thing many have seen before their death at my hands, and I'm overthinking a phone call. I need answers, and there's only one way to get them. Better do this now before I talk myself out of it.

Katarina's warning plays on repeat in my head, but I grab my phone and dial the number. I straighten my spine, wincing from the slight discomfort. I know I deserved the punishment, but being at the hands of that sadistic fuck, Vlad still doesn't sit right with me. He enjoyed hitting me. I feel myself getting angry all over again. Good.

The phone rings several times before a man with a deep, gritty voice picks up. "I expected an update days ago, Brian. Where is Kolinski, and who's involved?" Fuck. "Italian," I say through gritted teeth

"Russian and a woman, interesting. Is Brian still among the living?"

"Before we discuss Brian, I'd like to know what exactly you thought that piece of shit Kolinski was involved in. Sharing information would be beneficial to both of us."

"Yes, I'm sure you would. If we're going to be sharing information, I'd like to know whom I'm speaking to?" he says smoothly

"Okay. My name is Anya Gorbachev, your turn," I say.

It's risky giving him my real name, but at this point, I don't have any fucks left to give.

"Good evening, Miss Gorbachev, my name is Vincenzo

SARAH JANE

Gambino. Now that we have the formalities over, Brian was sent to watch Kolinski and report where he went and who he was speaking to." His voice is like a fine wine, and it puts me on edge.

"I know why he was here. I'd like to know what you believe Kolinski was into," I say, mildly irritated. I know avoidance when I hear it.

"Kolinski is suspected of kidnapping and dealing in sex trafficking of underage girls. We received word of two local girls being snatched and sold by Kolinski to a Russian from Vegas, so I had him followed to see who he met."

"Kolinski has been coming to our casino for a few months and frequenting our whore house. Got a little rough with one of the girls one too many times and unfortunately died staring at his dick." I almost add how much pleasure it gave me to do it.

"I see. That does cause a problem, Bella. I needed Kolinski alive to find out where and whom he sold those girls to."

"We don't deal in underage girls. My father would not allow it. Your intel must be wrong, Mr. Gambino."

"I have been very patient and forthcoming, do not do me the disrespect of calling me a liar. They were sold by Kolinski to a Russian in Vegas. I have a description of a man that works for your father, Miss Gorbachev. I just need a name and my associate returned to me."

"And I'm telling you that's not possible in all regards. Brian shared what he learned while here, which didn't indicate he knew who he was looking for, just that he observed Kolinski until he disappeared. He was about to give me your name before he was shot."

BABA YAGA

Pieces of the puzzle are falling into place, and I don't like it.

"You mean to tell me not only did you kill Kolinski, but you also killed an FBI agent? If you don't want an all-out war between our families, princess, you best find out where those girls are and get me a name," he seethes down the phone at me.

"War isn't necessary, Gambino. I'll look into this matter personally. In the meantime, write down this number, and send me all information you have obtained so far and everything on the girls as well." I rattle off the number to my burner.

"It will be done, and I expect results, Gorbachev. I'd hate to have to kill you and your family."

"You have no idea what I'm capable of. Don't threaten me."

"One more thing before you go, I have some of the best hackers in the world under my employ, and yet you got my number from a phone I was told couldn't be hacked. Not too many are capable of such skill. I'm intrigued." And with that, he hangs up.

My phone beeps with incoming messages, so I scroll through the information. Both girls are fourteen, have that youthful beauty, and are completely innocent. Still scrolling, I come to the description of the man Kolinski presumably sold the girls to. As I'm reading, my blood runs cold. Only one man fits the description given, and that means not only is he a traitor, but he has also broken one of our sacred rules. We don't harm children. The Bratva is ruthless, hard, and violent; however, Gorbachev's have

149

SARAH JANE

never touched children, and stealing them from the Italians is even stupider.

With Liam set to return in a few weeks for his fight, I must find those girls, collect evidence, and see that the Butcher pays for everything he's done.

CHAPTER 23

ANYA

Time is slipping by so quickly that I constantly feel like I'm racing to keep up. Liam is arriving in two days for the fight. In his absence, his emails have reminded me that there is good in this world.

I have gone down a dark hole, and I fear I may never find my way back. I'm grasping onto the living, so I don't get swallowed whole.

After discovering what Vlad has been up to, I have been so focused on my anger that Baba Yaga has taken over and very little of Anya remains. I've painted my room of death in so much blood it'll never come clean. Every time I've been called to deal with a problem, all I see are those girls' faces and Vlad's smug countenance thinking he's getting away with it. I lose control. Alexey is worried I'll go too far. He isn't wrong. I don't feel in control.

My father is tightening the reins on everything, making it harder for me to go unnoticed while following Vlad and now Sergei and Dmitry, as it seems they are taking orders from the wrong master. I made another trip to The Kitty House for Katarina's assistance, digging into Vlad's financials, properties, and anything that could give me a direction toward finding these girls and exposing him for the heinous piece of shit I always knew he was. The longer the girls are missing, the worse this situation becomes for them and my family.

Gambino is getting impatient, and I don't need the Italian mob showing up. It'll be a bloodbath with too many losses on both sides.

She was able to find a few warehouses in the industrial district linked to a shell company owned by the Butcher and trucking manifests of deliveries made to said buildings on several dates over the last six months. One date coincidentally matches the timeline of the disappearances, the arrival of Kolinski and then Brian. This doesn't prove anything, but it's worth looking into.

I've scoped out the area and found a rotating group of guards and a schedule of men coming and going from the building at night. The men must be paying customers, which only motivates me to get this done and soon.

Sasha and Katarina have both offered to be there to help the girls process what happened to them and start their journey to healing before they are returned home. I couldn't ask for better friends.

The best night to move on the building will be Liam's

BABA YAGA

fight, when everyone will be on hand with my father. I plan on being front and center when the bell rings to watch Liam become a champion. His opponent is Russian and a tough fighter, but I've watched firsthand the work Liam and his team have put in to prepare him for this fight, so I have faith he will win. I also have a few ideas on how we can celebrate, but business comes first.

I haven't seen Declan much since he stood by my hospital bed. I do know the "job" he was given is a load of shit, and he's racking up a debt he has no hope of repaying. He's managed to avoid running into me, though I have seen him leaving the whorehouse and stumbling onto the elevators late at night from the security offices. Declan told me to stay out of it and my father ordered me to back off when I asked too many questions. I can't see what the endgame is here. The only road this leads to is me and a shallow grave.

So many moving pieces and revelations that the lines are becoming blurry. When my world comes crashing down, I wonder who will be left standing and if I can live with the consequences.

LIAM

Two days. In two days, I'll be flying back to Vegas for my shot at a belt. These past weeks have been hard, pushing me further than ever and getting me to this point. I've worked, fought, sweat, and sacrificed for this. It comes down to five rounds in the cage with a tough fighter well-rounded in skill and the fiercest opponent I have ever faced. His record is an impressive 29-0, so leading up to this, Ronan, his father, Danvers, and the boys watched hours of his fights, breaking down his stance, moves, style, and technique to find anything for me to manipulate. Then they made me watch to see if I picked up what they did and if I found anything useful to exploit as well.

The guys took turns filming my training to see where we needed to improve and to send emails to Anya. Having her see me train and add her input has bolstered me to a level I didn't think I could reach. She adds confidence, and her belief that I will win makes me believe it as well. Some may think I'm crazy with how calm I seem right now, but knowing who is in my corner makes all the difference.

I sent the videos to my father, offering an olive branch as I still harbor some guilt over how things ended between us before I left. I received some advice, comments, and praise regularly for the first few weeks. Then he started to get sporadic, so I called and spoke to him on FaceTime to get a read on how he was doing.

Each time I see him he seems to be pulling further away. I can tell he's hitting the bottle despite his assurances that he loves the new job, not to worry because all is well, and he'll bloody drink after a long day if he fucking wants to. So nothing has changed, yet everything has. He's a grown-ass man, and I don't want to worry over him anymore, but old habits die hard. There will come a day when I have to walk away from him and be done. The reality is I worry that day is coming real soon.

CHAPTER 24

LIAM

Touching down in Vegas hits differently this time. I'm a different man, a man I finally think I can be proud of. We don't get the same reception this time around.

I'm sad Anya isn't here to greet me, but she assured me that I'll see her after the weigh-in and press conference.

A driver with a sign waits at the terminal, so we collect our luggage and follow him out to the limo. Everyone piles in, making small talk as we drive to Vice. The guys are pumped up, making bets on which round and how I'll win, while Ronan takes the piss and suggests I'll lose. He winks at me just as the boys get rowdy, causing me to laugh my ass off at the stupidity and loyalty of these brothers of mine. Bloody lunatics.

We're still chuckling as we walk into the hotel when

SARAH JANE

my father walks up, and all joking ceases. He looks like shit, thinner, sickly almost, his suit is wrinkled, and he smells like he hasn't bathed in a week. Don't get me started on the stench of booze.

"Hello, my boy, so glad to have you back," he says before giving me a quick hug and a pat on the back. "You look different but the same. I'm proud of you, Liam."

Stepping back, he smiles at me one more time before excusing himself to go do "business." I look at Ronan, and he looks concerned, slowly shaking his head. I don't have words, so I focus on what I know has to happen.

We're shown to the same rooms we had before, so I drop the guys off on their floor and proceed up to mine. The elevator brings back memories, and I'm smiling like a fool when I step off.

I want to knock on Anya's door. It's been too long since I've touched her. I need a taste like a starved man needs to eat, but I have weigh in and press in a few hours, and I need a power nap. The flight was long and exhausting.

Unlocking the door, I walk into a familiar space, unpack a few things, strip down to my shorts, and lie down on the bed for some shut-eye.

I wake a few hours later to my alarm blaring. Getting up, I stretch, already feeling better and ready to go. I walk into my bathroom, turn on the shower, hop in, and rinse off the day. I prepare myself for the conference and the usual smack talk that ensues. After wrapping a towel around my waist, I brush my teeth. Once I walk back into my room, I notice the note left on the nightstand.

Hello Handsome,

I didn't want to wake you, long flights are a bitch, so I watched you sleep for a bit before duty called. I've missed you, Liam more than I should admit. I'll see you tonight. XX

Your treasure, Anya

I could get used to that, but I know better than most that life happens, so I need to enjoy the moments in the present and not bank on tomorrow. Slipping on shorts and a T-shirt provided by my sponsors here at Vice- Anya's father- I slip on some flip-flops and head down to get my team.

Everything happens quickly and smoothly; we both make weight, pose for pictures, then move on to the conference portion. It's slow-moving after that. With the language barrier and needing a translator, the smack talk is almost comical. When translated back, you can tell the kid doesn't want to say some of the words, so the insults get lost. The boys and I are laughing by the time it's over, which sure beats being pissed off, considering some of the questions thrown my way about me lacking and how some find it insulting that I was offered the shot for the belt to begin with. I didn't sweat any of it; I answered calmly with a touch of sarcasm and moved on to the next question. I know he's a good fighter. I don't need reminding. I earned my seat at the table, and tomorrow night, everyone will know it too.

Mr. Gorbachev is here with the goons and the ugly

motherfucker. Yes, I'm still calling him that, and no, that won't change anytime soon. Anya and my father are both absent. One I know I'll see later, and the latter I have no clue.

The men make their way down to me after things wrap up. I still don't trust these men, but I shake hands, give thanks for the opportunity, and let them know I look forward to being the new champion, which earns me a weird look and a silent conversation I'm not privy to. Mr. Gorbachev wishes me good luck then they're gone in a blink of an eye.

Finn, Mac, and Patty suggest pasta, so once I change, I take them down to the Italian place Anya first took me to. We fill our stomachs with carbs, and it's just what I need. I laugh till my gut hurts before I bow out, letting them have a few drinks. I head back to my room and watch mindless TV for a couple of hours before giving up and heading to bed.

I'm just dozing off when I hear my door open and close, and then footsteps enter my room. I can smell her from the doorway, and my dick hardens. God knows I've missed her. She stops by the bed and undresses. I can make out her silhouette in the shadows from light slipping through the cracks in the curtains. She's beautiful. I just want to lie here and stare at her. She pulls back the covers and climbs into bed beside me. I can't wait any longer, so I reach for her and pull her till her body is flush with mine.

"Hello, my treasure," I whisper in her ear as I breathe in the lavender smell, feeling like I've finally come home.

She flinches, and a sharp gasp leaves her mouth, making me pull back and attempt to turn on the light.

"I'm okay, Liam. Leave the light. I just overdid it with

my workout this morning," she says quietly while reaching to place her hand on my cheek. "Kiss me, please. I've missed you."

I can't say no to that request, so I lower my head to place kisses along her collarbone, up her neck, and across her cheek. Then I take her lips slowly like we have all the time in the world. Her hand leaves my cheek to join the other roaming my back. I shake with need as her touch lights my skin on fire. We lie there in no rush before I pull back.

"You sure you're okay, love? Has anything happened while I've been gone?"

"Don't ruin this, please, Liam. Be here and now with me. We can face the ugly tomorrow, okay?" Grabbing my arms and nestling into my neck, she breathes in my smell.

I slowly move and turn her over so her back is to my chest. Gathering her up in my arms, I tell her what she needs to hear. "Okay love, sleep now. Tomorrow we'll fight the demons."

Her breathing evens out, and I lightly squeeze her and kiss the top of her head. Finally having her back in my arms, I let myself drift off. Tomorrow, I fight for my future and the woman lying in my arms.

CHAPTER 25

ANYA

I wake just before dawn, overheating from Liam's body wrapped around me. My injuries, although healed, are still stiff and sore, leaving me feeling vulnerable and not at my best. Liam asking questions right now won't bode well for anyone. He still has no idea who he's in bed with, literally and figuratively. I slowly slip from the bed and use the bathroom before quietly getting dressed. I need to be in my place should anyone come looking for me. I leave Liam a note that I'll see him later today for his fight, I need a new dress, I think to myself, and I'll be seated front and center to cheer him to victory. After quickly kissing his lips while he sleeps, I slip out the door.

No issues come up as I slip back into my place, but to be safe, I do a quick sweep making sure no listening devices or cameras have been installed in my absence. This mess with Vlad has me overly cautious. I didn't think anything he could do would surprise me, but I find myself disgusted more each day. Sasha reported to Alexey the Butcher has been on edge and extra rough with her the last few visits. She isn't the only one, but with Alexey trying to keep up the act of a loyal soldier, his hands are tied. He pays the girls more than usual for their silence and thanks the heavens that Katarina isn't Vlad's type. If Vlad's tastes ran that way, my friend would sign his death warrant in his pursuit of vengeance.

Everything is clear so I change into a pair of black wide-leg slacks, a blood-red silk blouse, and some light makeup, then pull my hair back in a ponytail. I have an important call to make and a day to get started. A huge knot in my gut tells me something will irrevocably change my life today.

I head back down to the kitchen to start some coffee and grab a quick bite of granola, yogurt, and fruit before heading to the office I had set up just off my living room while I was recovering. Katarina set up the computer system, giving me all the bells and whistles and top-notch security should anyone come looking.

Taking that first drink of coffee is pure heaven, in my opinion, and officially starts my day. Quickly downing it, I get all the paperwork I need and log into my computer. With a few clicks across the keyboard, the video chat window pops up and it starts to ring.

A few seconds pass before a face I'm meeting for the first time comes up on the screen.

"Good morning, Miss, Gorbachev. I assume you have

some news for me, or you wouldn't be stupid enough to call me." His thick Italian accent sounds stronger when he lacks patience.

"Anya, please, and you can stop with the idle threats. We both know damn well you looked into me and found I'm not lacking in any sense of the word. You don't scare me, Mr. Gambino." I say with as much sweetness as I can muster.

He tilts his head back and lets out a loud laugh. If I wasn't so hung up on my tattooed sexy-as-fuck fighter sleeping next door, I might be tempted to climb this man like a tree, consequences be damned. I'd wager he is 6'2", and his broad chest and shoulders fill out his three-piece tailor-made suit quite nicely. Add to that his dark, almost raven, hair, olive skin, and piercing eyes. Never thought I'd ever see a day where I could look at an enemy and feel lust or utter the words I wish to say to Liam.

"You are a breath of fresh air, Anya. I admire your grit; you are correct, I did look into you, and what I found well, Baba Yaga, your reputation precedes you. If I thought I could steal you and get away with it, I would. I could use someone with your skill set. Alas, it is not to be. Back to business. What do you have for me?"

"I found the warehouse where the girls are being held and, from my estimation, at least another dozen girls are there as well. How soon can you have a team ready to go for extraction? The best opportunity you will have is tonight."

"Fuck. Did you get eyes on the other girls? I can have the jet fueled and be in the air within the hour; however, I wasn't prepared to take fourteen girls," he says pursing his lips while color rises in his cheeks in anger.

"I realize that, but I need your word that you will get all of them out. I don't want his rage taken out on the girls left behind should you only grab your two."

"You have my word. It's inconvenient, but I would never leave children to suffer any more than they already have. I take it you have all the intel I need?"

"As I said, tonight is your best option. We have a very publicized title fight taking place, and everyone will be indisposed here. I will send you all the schematics of the building, best entrances to strike, camera locations, security rotations etcetera. If you hit just after dark, the security is lessened overnight so as not to garner attention. People don't come looking if it just looks like another warehouse with night guards. Bring your tech guy, the security will need to be highjacked and looped so you can get in and out." Opening another window, I send him all the files I have and hear the notification sound comes through on his end.

He opens it, and I watch him quickly scan the documents before picking up the phone on his desk. Punching in a number, he tells whoever is on the other end to get his brothers to his place stat, fuel the jet, gather six men and collect Nico from his dungeon. He hangs up and turns back to me.

"I will say I was a bit skeptical that you would hold up your end of the bargain. My experience with the Bratva has ended in bloodshed on both sides, however, you have my respect, Anya. I won't soon forget what you have done for me. You'll have to excuse me if I don't share the details of my arrival, we can't have any further complications."

"I agree it is best I know no further details, but I will ask to have confirmation and verification that all fourteen girls were retrieved and updates when they are returned to their families. If they should require counseling, I will be more than happy to provide that for them, discreetly, of course."

"I will send a message when we have all the packages and are safely back in the air. Thank you for the offer, however, we Italians take care of our own. I hope our next conversation will be a much more pleasant one." With that, he hangs up and my computer screen goes dark.

Next conversation? A thought for another time. I scrub the computer like Kat showed me and walk to the coffee pot for another cup. Sending prayers to whoever listens that the girls will be saved, and no long-lasting effects ruin their lives, I finish my cup and strap on my belt with a built-in holster for my knives.

They sit discreetly at my sides and are hidden by the black blazer I put on. To anyone looking, I'm the model businesswoman that works for her father.

Picking up my keys and my phone, I head out the door to the elevator. I'll do my rounds before heading to the morning meeting where we go over logistics for Liam's fight tonight.

As the elevator doors close, his face fills my mind, and I smile so wide my face hurts. I finally found something worth living for. Someone worth fighting for.

CHAPTER 26

LIAM

I woke up to the other side of my bed cold. She must've left early. I hope this doesn't become a habit with her disappearing before dawn. It seems weird to even hope that we form habits with each other, but it's there. I swing my legs over the side of the bed and head straight for the shower.

Mid-rinse, it hits me. This is it. Tonight is my shot. I've put in the work, never felt stronger or more focused in my career, and Anya has only made it better. Turning off the shower, I step out grab a towel and wrap it around my waist. I head out to the fridge for a bottle of water and slowly sip while silently wishing it was coffee. I swear off coffee during training, and the thought of having a cup tomorrow morning to celebrate my win sounds bloody brilliant, especially if my dark-haired siren is having one too.

SARAH JANE

A knock at the door gets my attention, and I can hear the daft bastards I call friends and brothers before I even have the handle turned.

"Room service, sir. Anything else I can do for you?" Mac says, rolling a food cart in

"Oh, yeah, we offer top-of-the-line service around here." Ronan wanders in, batting his eyes at me.

"Bloody idiots, the lot of you. Besides, we all know it's my rugged good looks that put your ugly mugs to shame," Patty throws in

"I can't believe I call you eejits friends," Finn follows, shaking his head.

I couldn't ask for better mates than this lot, so after I'm done chuckling, I ask, "What are you lot doing here?" I stroll over to lift a lid on the cart to find an omelet, orange juice, and a fruit bowl.

"What does it look like, you daft bastard? Fueling that lanky-ass body of yours for this fight tonight," Ronan says before taking a seat.

"Fair enough," I say. "And there ain't nothing lanky about this ass fucker." Chuckling, I sidestep into my room to throw on shorts and a T-shirt.

Sitting down, we all dig into our meals, and a peace I've never felt before a fight washes over me.

Finishing up, Ronan tells me to get my shit together so we can head down to the gym for some light warm-ups and grappling. We head to the elevator, and I can't help but look over to Anya's door. I can't wait to see her later at the fight; everyone who matters to me will be here to see me make my mark.

Getting down to the gym was easier this time, and the

boys are impressed with the setup. There's no siren in the cage this time, but my opponent is here, and the ugly fucker is by the cage watching. We watch for a few minutes and then head to the other end of the gym to get started.

Maksim Konstantin is a beast. Where Ivan was lanky and fast, Maksim is bulkier and more powerful in his strikes and kicks. He'll be harder to take down.

Ronan smacks my arm, telling me to focus. I shift to take one last look and catch the big ugly fucker smirking at me, which just pisses me off. Taking a quick deep breath, I calm my mind, and we get to work.

Fight days are usually light. It gets my mind and body on the same page by warming up with light sparring and running a few groundwork drills. Everything fades away while we work, and by the time Ronan calls time, I feel great and

prepared for this fight. The gym had cleared out, which makes me wonder if Maksim doesn't see me as a threat. If he doesn't that'll be his mistake.

The day passes by in a blur. We go over and over the game plan and watch more footage of Maksim's previous fights, helping me pick apart his weak spots, go-to moves, and so on. His right is his dominant side, but he can throw a good left hook if needed, so my guard will always need to be up. He's a sucker for a combo and uses his bulk well. All his wins are by knockout, and his ground game is my way in for the win. I need to be faster, take his ass to the mat, and keep him there.

With the work done, it's time to kick some ass in Call of Duty. The lads slowly trickle out, heading to take showers and get changed, leaving Ronan and me.

SARAH JANE

"Are you ready for this, Liam?" he asks, looking at me the way his father does when he's serious and invested in what you have to say.

"Honestly, I've never felt so calm before a fight. I prepared, I did the work, I feel confident I can win, and that's what I need to focus on."

"What do you think the difference is this time?"

"My life has changed for the better. I mean, Dad is doing god knows what, but it's been nice not having to carry all the weight of his shit. I met Anya, and I finally feel like I've met my equal in all ways, and my career has led me to all this and my chance for a title, so I'm counting my blessings."

"I'm happy for you, Liam. Just be careful, okay? Whatever Declan is doing isn't good. We both know it, and Anya is great, but there are still too many unanswered questions surrounding her family and that ugly fucker who watches her. It unsettles me and not much does. You earned this fight, and I can't wait to be in your corner tonight when you win. Don't lose sight of that." With that, Ronan gets up and heads out the door to get ready as well, leaving me to my thoughts.

Time flies by in a blur until it's time to head to the locker rooms. I still haven't seen Anya, but she sends a few sporadic texts saying she's getting ready and will see me there. Gathered in the locker room, we talk shit and make bets on each round, with the loser buying the first two rounds. It's our calm before the storm, or it was till my father walks in looking like life chewed him up and spat him out. He attempts to smooth out his wrinkled tie and shirt before he clears his throat.

168

BABA YAGA

"I need a minute with my son, fellas before he goes out," he says with a slight wobble to his words.

Nobody moves as we can't quite process what we're looking at

"Now!" he yells

I nod to the guys, and they file out the door. Ronan lingers to give me a look and shuts the door behind him.

"What's this all about, Dad, and why do you look wrung out?"

He starts pacing back and forth. If he keeps it up, he's going to put a hole in the floor.

"Liam I-" He starts. "I'm... I, ugh, I'm so sorry. I'm so stupid. I just thought it might be different."

"Dad, stop fucking pacing and start making sense. What have you done, and do we need to be discussing this now?" I ask, trying to keep the irritation out of my voice. He probably needs money again.

"Never mind. Whatever you have to say to me can be said after my fight. I can't deal with your shit right now."

Getting up, I make my way to the door to show him out when he blurts, "I need you to throw the fight, Liam."

"What did you just fucking say to me?"

"You heard me. Please don't make me repeat it."

I stalk toward him, backing him up till his back hits the locker, and fear creeps into his eyes.

"I'm going to ask you again what you said, and your answer better be different."

"I fucked up, Liam, and I'm in too deep. You don't fuck with these people, Liam. It's toe the line, or I'm a dead man."

"Who's they, and how much do you owe?" I'm

seething, and never have I wanted to hit my father as much as I do in this moment.

"Anya's father, Mr. Gorbachev, is a dangerous man; you can't buy me my way out of this, Liam. This was set up from the start. The price is you throwing the fight or I'm dead."

He reeks of whiskey, cigarettes, and piss. He's scared, and I'm spiraling out of control as my whole world comes crashing down around me. All the signs were there, it just sounded too good to be true. I don't want to believe my father would do this to me, but powerful men find the weak link and use it to force their will time and again.

"Get out. I don't ever want to look at your face again. You are dead to me, Da." He doesn't move, but I can feel him crumble as he starts to cry.

"I said get out!" slamming my hand against the nearest locker.

"I'm so sorry, son. I didn't mean-"

"You never do, and I'm not your son," I manage to say

The door slams open with all my best mates looking from Declan to me and back. He keeps mumbling "I'm sorry" as tears track down his face, and walks out the door without a glance back.

"Well, I guess I'll be the one to ask, what just happened, Liam?" Finn, the usually quiet one of the group, speaks up, earning looks from the other three before they all look at me for an answer.

I can't tell them; I know what they'd say. The only wild card would be Ronan. He's been with me the longest and knows every dark, dingy hole I've had to pull Declan out of. His loyalty is to me, but I can't let them kill my father.

Baba Yaga

I've never felt so defeated. Slapping a fake-ass grin on my face is my best bet here until it's over.

"Same old bullshit." I shrug it off.

A knock sounds at the door still open from the cavalry storming in. "O' Conner you're up."

Cheers go up, and they slap me on the back before filing back out the door. I follow and almost smack into Ronan. Should've known he'd know.

"When this is done, we are having words, you and I. You're going to tell me what the fuck Declan has done, Liam. You hear me?"

"Yeah, I hear you. We'll talk when it's done." And I walk out the door, ready to throw my life away to save the eejit I once called my dad.

CHAPTER 27

ANYA

My day has been a whirlwind. After my early morning phone call, I've run interference all over the hotel and casino. If I didn't know better, I'd say keeping me busy was the plan. The morning meeting was strained with Declan in attendance, still pretending he has an actual job here. He refused to make eye contact with me, and the smug look on Vlad's face had the hair on the back of my neck up. My father was very short and brief with expectations on operations running smoothly today, getting everything in place for the fight tonight. VIP clients, senior Bratva members, and their entourage, politicians in our pocket, and contacts my father hopes to develop relationships have all arrived. Getting everyone to their rooms and catering to their needs for wives, mistresses, and hookers had my morning booked solid.

Just after lunch, I saw Vlad escorting Declan down a back hallway to receiving, but when I made to follow, Sergei popped up with a security issue in the casino. Seems one of our VIPs neglected to turn over his firearm upon arrival, and a few locals in for an afternoon of cards were very uncomfortable. We have the best security here, and I pride myself on it. With a little finesse and ego stroking, the man handed over his weapon, and I gave everyone a free round of drinks at the table, smoothing things over.

Passing Alexey on my way to the security office to hand in the gun for safe- keeping, he slips something in my hand and keeps walking without a word. Casually slipping the note into my pocket, I walk into the main security office and hand in the weapon, get an update on all areas, send a report to my father's phone, and head to the dress shop and spa before I get detained yet again. Sending Liam, a quick text to let him know I'm getting ready, and I'll see him soon, I slip into our resident dress shop and walk past a few ladies getting dressed for this evening. I nod to the girl at the counter before heading into the back area in search of Antoinette, the genius in-house designer.

"Perfect timing as always, Anya. I finished the last details this morning, I must say, this is the most detailed exquisite dress you've commissioned from me," she exclaims while walking to the black dress bag hanging up on a panel of a beautiful, ornate screen divider in the corner.

Antoinette is the most elegant woman I know. At sixty-five, she is a timeless beauty with classic features, and

SARAH JANE

minimal makeup, and wears her long blond hair in a braided bun swept away from her face. She is the only person I know who still remembers my mother besides my father. I imagine they would've been ageless beauties and great friends had my mother survived.

"Come, child, slip behind here, and I'll hand you the dress. I wish to see it on you"

I won't deny her this, and I am eager to see if my vision looks as good as it did in my head when I ordered it. Slipping out of everything but my thong, she hands me the dress and a pair of gold stilettos. Everything in place and shoes on, I step around the screen and meet Antoinette's teary eyes.

"Oh, my sweet girl. You look so much like your mother at this moment." Dabbing her eyes, she turns. "Come see for yourself."

There is nothing sweet about me, it was broken out of me long ago, but some part of me craves the reference to my mother, whose memory is slipping further away every year. Walking to the mirror, I get my first look, and my breath catches. It's perfect.

"You truly are a genius, Antoinette. It is perfection."

Turning from side to side, I admire the sweetheart neckline with off-the-shoulder chiffon off the cuffs, the corset-like boning brings in my waist and the full beautiful skirt with hidden pockets in a gorgeous emerald green. Exquisite gold embroidery details, simple and subtle, grace the gown, and black satin lines it for a two-tone effect.

I feel truly beautiful at this moment. I can pretend I'm not a killer, not tainted by evil. I'm just a woman wearing a dress to watch her man win a fight. He's not meant to be

BABA YAGA

mine, but I'm being selfish for the first time in my life. I want him, and until this second, I wasn't so sure about my decision. I'm owed some happiness. I've earned it, and God help anyone who gets in my way. I take one last look before changing back into my clothes.

"Can you have that delivered to my suite, Antoinette?"

"Of course, Anya, it would be my pleasure. Whatever decision you just made, I almost feel bad for anyone who tries to stop you." She winks before kissing both my cheeks and sending me on my way.

Just before I enter the salon, I remember the note Alexey handed me. Turning my back to the camera in the hall, I pull it out of my pocket and lean against the wall pretending to check my phone.

Timetable has moved up, overheard Butcher promising product before the fight, they are going to be moved, update our friend he needs to move quicker. Also, something is going down with Liam's father. I'm digging. Will send an update when I know more. Be careful Anya I don't have a good feeling about this.

Well fuck. Pulling up the number, I hold the phone to my ear. It rings twice and goes to voicemail.

"Good afternoon, sir. This is Miss Gorbachev calling to

175

let you know the VIP guests you requested for this evening have been made available sooner. So if you would be agreeable to moving your party up, we can accommodate that. Please let me know at your earliest convenience. Thank you."

This day is going to shit already. I hope this message gets to him in time because this is our only chance at saving these girls without a full-out war starting. As for Liam's father, I'll track him down after my appointment. I think it's time we have ourselves a chat.

Decisions made, I head in to get my hair done and a manicure and pedicure, with my last stop to have my makeup applied. This is a big event, and my father has very high expectations. Appearances are everything. Feeling ready for the masses, I leave to get changed and go see Declan before the fight.

I had the hairstylist sweep half my hair up in curls and pin it in place with the rest cascading down my back. I can't wear my kunai knifes with this dress so I opt for ornate diamond-encrusted chopsticks strategically placed to look like the decoration in my hair but readily available as a weapon should I need it. Finishing touches in place, I pick up my keys and my phone, slip them both into the hidden pockets of my dress, and proceed to the elevator pressing the button for one floor down to collect Liam's wayward father for the fight.

The elevator doors ping, and when they open, I'm not looking at an empty hall but into the eyes of Dmitry and Alexey.

"Excuse me, I'm here to collect Declan for the fight." I

BABA YAGA

try to sidestep Dmitry who has yet to move, so I turn to Alexey.

"Is there a problem?"

"No problem, Anya. It seems Mr. O'Conner isn't here, but it will be our pleasure to escort you down to the fight," Alexey says, tight-lipped.

"How kind of you," I return dryly.

Both men step onto the elevator. Dmitry positioned himself in front of me and Alexey beside me.

Alexey squeezes my right hand, and that bad feeling I've had all day is now screaming in the pit of my stomach. When we hit the ground floor, Sergei is waiting for us, and the feeling gets much worse. He steps in beside me after I exit the elevator, essentially boxing me in as we make our way to the fight.

Preliminaries have started when we arrive, and I'm escorted to the elaborate area my father has blocked off for his guests.

Handshakes, small talk, and introductions are made as I make my way to my father, who is in deep conversation with a man I don't recognize. Taking my seat, I order a drink and start scanning my surroundings for anything that doesn't fit. This feels all wrong. From the corner of my eye, I see Vlad enter with Declan in tow, looking like a dead man walking. They disappear down the back hallway toward the locker room. I set my drink down and go to stand when a hand touches my shoulder and pushes me back into my seat.

"Don't move, Anya. Your father is watching. Smile, face forward, and put that mask of yours back on. I will go find out what's going on," Alexey says, patting my shoulder and moving away.

He knows better than to touch me without permission. In this instance, though, he means to help and not hinder me. I respect Alexey even if I ultimately find him weak, so I look over to my father, who does indeed have one eye on me. I raise my glass and smile, which is returned then turn my attention back to the fight, keeping one eye on the hallway they went down.

Vlad comes back out, grinning in the sinister way he does. That doesn't bode well for anyone. A few minutes later, Alexey escorts Declan out, looking defeated with tears tracking down his face. I get a slight head shake when I meet Alexey's eyes, and they disappear out the back door.

"Face forward, Anya, that doesn't concern you. I suggest you start minding your own business, princess," Vlad says, materializing beside me and then taking the seat beside me.

"Ah, Vlad, when are you going to learn I don't give a fuck what you think" I reply sweetly.

He grabs my left arm, squeezing hard enough to make me flinch

"Don't push me, you little bitch, or the first lesson I'll teach you in obedience will be cutting your tongue out so you can't talk at all."

"Get your fucking hand off me, Vlad, or I will finish what my father started on your face." Pulling my arm from his grasp, I smooth the skirt of my dress.

Hearing the start of Galway Girl over the loudspeakers, I paste on my best smile and turn to see Liam make his entrance.

BABA YAGA

I refuse to let Vlad ruin this for me. I can feel him aiming daggers at the back of my head, but I don't care. I just want to see Liam. Patty, Finn, Mac, and Ronan walk out first, getting the crowd going for their friend.

Liam finally comes into view. He's smiling and doing all the right things, but something is off. When he gets closer to the cage, I can see the tension in his body, the set of his jaw. He goes through the motions of undressing down to his shorts, having his gloves checked, Vaseline placed by the cut man, and his mouth guard put in. He walks into the cage, goes to his area, and starts scanning the crowd till he finds me.

I smile at him, hoping his panty-dropping smirk will appear, but it doesn't. Instead, he looks to my left where Vlad is still sitting. I turn to look as well, and Vlad has a shit-eating grin on his face. Fuck, fuck, fuck. I turn back to Liam, and he glances at me one last time before turning to his opponent that just entered the rink.

The darkness inside me is raging to be let loose. I'm ready to burn this fucking building to the ground, loyalty be damned. The fucking bratva be damned. Whatever scheme or plan my father had for Liam has come to pass. I didn't stop anything.

I'm numb, feeling I've just lost the one thing I've ever truly wanted.

The referee goes over the rules, and both fighters touch gloves before resuming their stances. The horn sounds, and the crowd is so loud, screaming and chanting as Liam and Maksim circle each other.

I'm on the edge of my seat when Maksim clocks Liam with a right hook that visibly shakes him. *Why wasn't his guard up?* Ronan barks orders at him, but Liam ignores him, throwing a weak left that Maksim easily deflects. They throw punches back and forth, with Liam rarely making contact. I know this man, after watching all the training videos, he's not even trying.

It all starts to make sense. Declan owes my father, and this is the cost of doing business. It's nagging me, though. Why get Liam to throw a fight you got him into? My phone starts vibrating in my pocket. When I pull it out, there's a text message from a private number. I open the message, and it reads,

> Miss Gorbachev, I just wanted to thank you for your service and hospitality during my brief stay. The entertainment we procured was top-notch, and the party went off without a hitch. Should you ever need anything don't hesitate to call. I will send referrals and references for you when I arrive back in the office. - G

He got them. The girls are safe. Now I just must save a bull-headed fighter who probably thinks I know what is going on.

Looking back to the cage, Liam is bleeding from his left eye and his lip, yet he still isn't pushing forward. The horn sounds, sending both men to their corners.

Liam gets his eye checked, followed by his lip. He's cleaned up and cleared to go. Both men stand, and the cage empties.

BABA YAGA

Once the new round starts, Liam throws a punch-leg-kick combo which lands hard, shocking Maksim, who then charges Liam and pins him to the side of the cage. Vlad is laughing beside me.

"Get out of there, get out of there," I'm muttering repeatedly.

Maksim leans in real close like he's saying something to Liam. In the next second, Liam gets out of the hold, spins, and starts swinging as if his life depends on it, like he's possessed because he's not stopping even when the horn goes off. When the referee tries pulling him off, Liam hits him as well. Ronan climbs over the top of the cage, followed by Patty. They grab Liam by the arms and start pulling him toward the cage door. Finn and Mac are trying to keep the masses back as the crowd goes nuts. Our security floods through the doors to contain it before it becomes a riot. I look back at my father, who is stone cold calm while all his associates cheer, loving the show.

I stand to leave. I have to find Liam. Vlad is no longer beside me. He must've left during the commotion. Warning bells are going off, and I'm looking everywhere, noting Sergei, Dmitry, and Alexey are all missing as well.

"Anya." My father calls my name, but I can't look at him.

He can't have my obedience right now, so I pretend I don't hear him and head down the stairs from the VIP area. I push my way through the still-screaming crowd.

Maksim is being treated by Viktor in the cage. He's unconscious and bleeding a lot.

Security pushes people back to make a path for me. Wouldn't look good letting the boss's daughter get hurt.

SARAH JANE

Idiots. When I get to the tail end, I break out in a run, heading straight to the locker room Liam was assigned.

Breaking through the door, I find Ronan pacing pulling on his hair. Patty is on his phone, trying to call someone with no luck. He's agitated, hanging up and trying again.

"Where's Liam, Ronan?" I ask.

He spins on his heel, stalking across the room.

"What the fuck have you done with him, Anya? And where's Declan?" He's fuming.

"If I knew where he was, I wouldn't ask you, fucking idiot"

"Both of you knock it off. Having a pissing contest won't find my friend. Now, calm your tits and help me," Patty screams while still attempting to call someone who is not answering. "Declan's phone is going straight to voicemail."

Finn and Mac run into the locker room.

"We went to Declan's room, no answer, so we kicked the door in. He's gone. All his clothes, everything. It's like he was never there. We can't get to the penthouse floor without Liam's key card," Mac blurts out, trying to catch a breath.

"This is bad, Ro" Finn adds.

"They can't have disappeared into thin air," Ronan yells

I whistle, getting everyone's attention. "What happened after the fight? Let's retrace a few steps."

Patty opens his mouth first. "We don't know what the hell happened. Liam doesn't fight like that, and he would never hit a man when he's down. It doesn't make sense. When we grabbed him from the cage, he was talking in riddles, something about his dad. When we got back to the locker room, he lost it. Said we needed to find his dad now. He's never acted this irrationally, so Finn and Mac went up to the rooms. I went to the casino, and Ronan went to the front desk, but something didn't sit right when I found Ronan back in the lobby, so we hightailed it back here finding Liam gone along with his bag and clothes."

My phone picks that moment to vibrate. I look down, and it's a message from Alexey. One word:

Downstairs

All color drains from my face, and I start to back from the room. This can't be happening.

"Where do you think you're going? Who messaged you, Anya" Ronan stalks towards me.

"I can't explain what I don't know, but I need you to trust me. I don't deserve it, but I'm asking anyway, okay?"

Taking a deep breath, I pull my key card to the penthouse floor.

"Here's the key to the penthouse floor. Gather all of Liam's things if they're still there, then grab all of your stuff, go to the front desk, and calmly ask the girl for the keys to the courtesy vehicle. Then drive it to the southeast loading docks and wait for me there."

"What the fuck do you mean go get clothes, grab a vehicle, where the hell are you going?"

Tempers are starting to flare, and I need them to do what I ask. "I'm going to find Liam."

"I'm coming with you," Ronan interrupts.

SARAH JANE

"You can't, Ronan. Vlad will kill you on sight. I don't know what's going on, but this has his name all over it." I'm trying to be patient.

"Maybe we should listen to her, Ro," Finn pipes up.

The other two glare at both of us.

"This whole mess is because of her," Ronan screams in my face while pointing his finger.

"Get that finger out of my face before I break your hand. We're in this mess because Declan is fucking weak and couldn't say no to the drink and the money. At this point, who fucking cares. As long as I can find them before his stupidity costs us, Liam." I feel out of breath, but I'm done arguing. "I'm leaving."

"Find him, Anya."

I take one last look at his family and his friends. "You have my word. Now go and be ready to move."

Once I reach my office, I run to the closet in my bathroom, take off the dress at lightning speed, and throw on black leggings, a sports bra, and a T-shirt. I also grab my backup knives and tuck them into the custom pocket in the waistband at my back, easy to reach but not noticeable to the naked eye. I pull all the pins from my hair and pull it up into a ponytail, reinserting the chopsticks just in case. Leaning over the sink, I gulp deep breaths trying to calm my racing heart. This has to be my best performance yet. In, out, in, out. I can do this for him. I can do this.

Weapons ready, and mask in place, I walk over to the panel behind my desk and push. I then enter the code and wait for the door to open. Once they do, I descend the stairs into my room of death.

BABA YAGA

Alexey is holding Declan by the arm. He's banged up and looks like he pissed himself, but he's breathing.

Coming into the main space, the sounds of fists meeting flesh fills the air long before I see Sergei and Dmitry standing sentinel while the Butcher pounds his fists into anywhere he can reach on Liam's torso or face as he's tied to a chair. His face is barely recognizable.

I let out a breath which is louder than I mean to, getting Sergei's attention. "Boss," he says.

The punching stops with Vlad turning to face me.

"Ah, Baba Yaga. Just in time. I was just warming him up for you." Vlad sneers at me.

"Anya?" Liam spits blood, trying to lift his head.

I knew I couldn't keep him, but I wanted to, I wanted to be anything other than the boogeyman that snuffed out people's lives. I was kidding myself. I am Baba Yaga, and this is how I fall.

CHAPTER 28

LIAM

What have I done? I've just killed my father. I had a plan; I was going to throw my career down the toilet. I entered the cage knowing I was walking out with my dreams in tatters. I scan the crowd looking for Anya. I need to see her face, her eyes. I need to know if she knew if I'm a bigger fool than I already feel like. I find her looking like the queen she is, wearing a beautiful green dress with gold details. When our eyes meet, the biggest smile I've ever seen lights up her face. She's good at hiding her emotions, however, smiling isn't her go-to expression, so I'm confused. The ugly fucker is beside her, wearing a shit-eating grin, making me grind my teeth. Should've known he was involved. I'll take great pleasure in punching him in the fucking face if I make it out of this mess.

I turn back to my opponent. It's time to get this shit-show going.

BABA YAGA

As the first round starts, we circle each other. Maksim lands a right hook that rings my bell and splits my eyebrow. Blood runs down my face already. I take a few swings, but my heart isn't in it, and he deflects easily. It's hard to believe this is where I would end up. Another hit to my face splits my lip, and my vision is blurry from the blood. The horn goes off, giving me some respite.

We both head to our corners. The cut man comes to check my eye, which is almost closed, and treat the cuts. He asks questions, and I vaguely answer. When satisfied, he clears me to continue and walks out. Ronan barks at me with colorful and animated vocabulary, and I'd honestly laugh if I wasn't gutted to my very core.

Time's up, so everyone leaves the cage, and the horn blows to start the second round. I need to look like I'm at least trying, so I push, landing a punch followed by a leg kick to his side. It landed hard, Maksim is shocked for split second, then he charges me, backing me right up to the cage and pinning me in.

"Just get it over with," I say. I'm done.

He leans closer to my ear. "How does it feel to be owned, little man? I'm insulted for wasting my time on you. Maybe the Butcher will let me have a taste of that sweet bitch once he's done breaking her. Too bad you won't be around long enough to see it." He chuckles.

I see red. My control snaps and I lose it. I use the cage for momentum, pushing Maksim just enough for me to get out of his grip, spin, and start swinging. And I don't stop, not when the horn blows, not when the ref pulls me off. He takes a shot to the face for his trouble. The fog starts to clear when Ronan and Patty grab my arms and pull me off the guy. I don't know if he's still breathing or if I just killed a man. There isn't time to think about it.

It's mayhem. The crowd is going nuts, and security floods the place. Finn and Mac clear a path to get me out of here, pushing and shoving anyone in the way. Coming back to my senses, I'm taken over by dread

"Find my dad find my dad," muttering over and over.

I'm bleeding, and the adrenaline rush is crashing fast. The urgency to find my dad is overwhelming me. I've signed his death warrant. I need to get to him first.

"You're not making sense, Liam. Hold on. We're getting you out of here," Patty screams in my ear.

It's so loud, it's deafening until silence descends as we get into the hallway to my locker room.

"Jesus, Liam, what have you done? What the hell happened out there?" Ronan asks after they help me sit down on the bench.

Finn grabs his bag, puts on gloves, and starts grabbing bandages, and a suture kit to clean up my eye and close up the wound.

"Ro, you need to find my dad," is all I can manage

"We will find your dad after we talk."

"No, I need you to find him right now," I yell, coming off the bench.

With his palms up, Ronan looks at the other guys before looking back at me.

"Okay, Liam, Mac, Patty, and I will go look while Finn fixes you up, okay?"

"No, I need you all to go. They're going to kill my father if they find him. Please find him. I'll get changed and meet you in the lobby."

After a second to digest, Finn tapes a bandage to my face to help stop the bleeding before standing. "That should hold till we figure out how deep of a shithole we're in." He throws the gloves in the trash. "Let's go. I want the hell out of here."

"Thank you, all of you." Feeling weak is not something I'm used to. I haven't been weak since I was a boy.

"Don't thank us yet, Liam. We have to find Declan first," Patty says with sadness.

The door shuts behind them, and I let out the longest breath. My shoulders shake as I fight back tears. If he's dead, it's my fault, and I'll have to live with that for the rest of my life.

I turn around grabbing my bag from the locker. I'm pulling my shirt out when the door opens behind me

"That was quick, did you find him?" I say over my shoulder.

"I think you should be more worried about yourself," a thick Russian accent sound behind me.

I spin around but not quick enough to avoid the fist that flies at my face, and everything goes black.

A slap to my face has me coming to in a circular room strapped to a chair. I can only see out of one eye now, but from what I can see it has different equipment in places around the room. A table runs along one wall with things I don't think are toys laying on them. Taking in who is in here with me, I see the two stooges that were with Anya at the airport. On my right, Alexey is standing with an iron grip on my father's arm. He's been worked over well.

"Dad are you ok?" attempting to get out of the bindings

holding me down. He just whimpers and won't look me in the eye.

"You should be more worried about yourself right now, little man."

I know that voice.

Vlad slowly removes his suit jacket and tosses it on the floor. He rolls up the sleeves of his button-up shirt. "I'm going to enjoy killing you"

The first punch lands on my injured side, and I'm fighting to stay conscious but barely

"You couldn't be a good little dog and do as you're told." Smack.

"We are not people you fuck with."

Smack. A hard punch breaks a rib or two.

I'm gasping for air but never knowing when to shut up, I spit blood on his shoe and say, "What's the problem, you ugly fuck? Had to tie me down instead of fighting me like a man." I'm goading him, I know I am. if I'm going to die, it'll be on my terms.

His nostrils flare before he rains down blow after blow. I'm bleeding all over the floor. I don't even know where it's coming from. My energy is spent just trying to withstand the punches, drifting in and out. I won't last much longer.

My thoughts drift to Anya and how her smile lights up her whole face. We won't have that future I wanted. I wonder if my death will affect her, and I wish I could see her one last time. The punching finally stops. I slump over as pain radiates everywhere. So I'm still in the land of the living.

"Boss," goon number one says.

BABA YAGA

"Ah, Baba Yaga. Just in time, I was just warming him up for you," Vlad purrs at whoever joined the party.

Who the fuck is Baba Yaga?

"Since you're still breathing, it's only fitting she'll be the one to end your life," he says, chuckling. "Take a look at the boogeyman." Grabbing my chin, he lifts my head to face my maker.

Anya stands there as if I conjured her from thin air.

"Anya." Spitting blood, I choke out the words.

What is she doing here? And why is he calling her that name? Is she going to kill me? That can't be right.

"What is going on, Vlad? Why is Liam here? We don't kill the investments; we kill the motivation. My father won't be pleased with this turn of events" Anya enunciates slowly.

I'm well and truly done now. The last betrayal. I slump back over and wait for my death.

"Your little pet had an order and disobeyed. Your father demands respect, and I was all too happy to rectify that. Now get your weapon of choice, Anya. I want to be entertained."

———

ANYA

"Patience has never been a virtue you possess, Vlad," I purr at him, praying I sound convincing.

Liam is tied to the chair like so many before him in the center of the room covering the drain. He's bleeding every-where, barely conscious. I want to go to him, but if this is going to work, I have to sell this. I look to Alexey holding the broken man who once was Declan. Bleeding and dirty, he just stands there sobbing and mumbling incoherently. Alexey holds his expression, meeting my eyes. I can see the remorse there. If he could've warned me, I know he would have. I guess we are all being taught lessons today.

Putting my back to them, I walk to the table with my weapons and strap my knife holsters to each leg. I take one last deep breath, holding my hands in front of me to get the shaking to stop. These hands have caused so much death, covered in blood that will never come clean. My sins are etched in tattoos up my arms, never to wash away.

I'm not walking out of this room alive, but he will live, and that's enough for me. Turning around, I glance at my friend and wink.

"Liam, "MO GHRÀ THU, MO STÒR." *You are my love, my treasure.*

Grabbing my first knife, I aim and throw. Hitting Vlad in the leg, I grab another, throwing and hitting his shoulder. I run right at them, sidestepping Vlad and knocking him off balance before stepping up on Liam's leg, jumping in the air, and flipping over his head.

Sergei rushes me first, swinging and just missing my face. As I duck, I pull a knife and slice him across his abdomen. Dmitry grabs me from behind as Sergei bellows, putting pressure on his wound. Swinging my head back as hard as I can, I almost see stars when it connects with his nose with a crunch. He releases me instantly. I face him while smirking and kick him in the balls. When he hits his knees, I wrap one arm tightly around his neck with the other holding the opposite side of his face.

BABA YAGA

Leaning in, I whisper, "Dasvindaniya" and break his neck.

Sergei lets out a roar, running at me. Pulling out a knife, I let it fly and hit him in the shoulder. He's distracted long enough for me to grab the gun in his waistband, and I bring it down on the back of his head. He crumples to the ground, out cold. He should've shot me when he had the chance.

I slice through Liam's wrist restraints. "Get your legs out. I'll get Declan." I place a knife in his hand.

Pulling out the gun, I point it at my friend. Nobody can know or think he helped me. I mouth the word Sorry and shoot him in the shoulder. He releases Declan, and I hit him over the head, knocking him out as well. Grabbing Declan before he crumples proves difficult.

"Leave me here, Anya. Save my son," he cries.

"I'm not leaving you here. Now get up"

Laughing fills the air. "Ah, *Printsessa*, now you have a choice to make."

Vlad is holding Liam by the throat with one hand and the knife in the other. "I'm not stupid. None of us is walking out of here, Butcher," I spit at him "You're right. I'll weep for you at your funeral, Anya."

Liam makes a gurgling noise as Vlad cuts him from shoulder to waist.

Dropping Declan and the gun, I pull two more knives. "Let's dance, you and I."

"That won't be necessary, daughter." Anatoli comes into view "Never would I think you'd betray me or the Bratva. What a mess. Your fate will be decided by the council. Vlad kill the boy and his father. I will deal with your actions later."

193

SARAH JANE

"Gladly." Placing the knife at Liam's throat, Vlad prepares to kill the man I love. "Stop this, father! Please, I'll bargain for his life," I plead with him.

"You have nothing to bargain with, Anya."

"My life for his. I will submit in all ways; I will never speak his name or see him again. I will give myself to Vlad when the time comes willingly. Spare his life, and I submit mine."

I thank God Liam isn't conscious to argue about this. We are out of options.

"We both know Vlad needs me to take your place, and if you kill him, I will burn this fucking palace of yours to the ground. What will it be?"

Pondering my words, he looks at me with intensity. I can see pride and respect in his eyes. "You understand what this means?"

"Da"

"Very well. Vlad, release him. Alexey, so glad you could join us, take Liam. It's time he leaves." His tone demands obedience.

Vlad growls in anger and drops Liam to the ground. I rush to his side, helping him to his feet.

"Don't do this love. Please don't do this." he's grabbing my face, trying to look me in the eye.

"I need you to live, I'm sorry."

Alexey comes up beside me. "I've got him, Anya. Let go"

Liam slumps into Alexey's side, allowing Alexey's good arm to wrap around him, holding him up. They head to the door. Liam struggles to walk but keeps trying to turn back.

"What about my father," Liam asks, turning back to Anatoli.

"He isn't part of the bargain, Liam. In fact, do watch, should you have any thought of coming back here again."

Walking to me, he hands me a gun. My price has been paid.

I point the gun at Declan's head, he finally looks up at me. "Thank you for saving my son," he whispers before he closes his eyes.

I look at Liam one last time and tell him, "I love you, Liam."

Then I pull the trigger, killing his father.

He starts to pull at Alexey, fighting to come back. Even one-armed Alexey has more strength and drags him from the room calling my name.

Falling to my knees, I stare at the gun in my hands. Vlad gets Sergei up and heads to the door. I will pay for killing Dmitry, and Vlad will take great pleasure in my pain. My father's shoes come into view.

"Count yourself lucky you still have your life, Anya."

Standing up I pull my shoulders back and look my father in the eyes. "You should've killed me. One day soon, you might wish you did."

Giving him my back, I walk towards the stairs to my office.

"Of that, I have no doubt, Anya," he says Liam is alive, and Baba Yaga is no more. A new kind of monster is born.

To Be Continued...

Epilogue

Liam

"She killed him," I mutter in shock as Alexey drags my ass down the hallway. "She's a killer, my father is dead."

"She just forfeited her life for yours, Liam. You might want to be more grateful," Alexey grits out.

"I can't muster the energy to care," I mumble.

My emotions are all over. I can't reconcile the woman I love to the woman I just saw kill two people, including my father, remaining calm.

Crashing through the double doors to a receiving area, I see a black SUV outside the service entrance. All four doors open, and my friends come running.

Finn reaches me first. "Jesus, Liam, you're a mess. I don't know what to treat first." He presses in a few areas slowly. "Where's Declan?" he asks.

BABA YAGA

"He's dead," I manage, overcome with grief.

"And Anya?" Ronan says, looking back to the entrance.

"Anya made a deal, her life for his, so take your friend and get the hell out of here." Alexey lets go of me, giving me to Mac and Patty while Finn continues assessing me. He's losing blood from where Anya shot him.

"I'm coming back for her," I muster. I won't leave her to that fate.

"You better, now get out of here." He makes to leave but pauses. "You're going to need help; this is going to be war, and you will need to go to the darkest parts of your soul to win it." He reaches into his pocket and hands me a burner. "There's a New York number saved in that phone. Call it. Goodbye, Liam."

Alexey walks away, and I'm all but carried to the SUV and laid in the backseat. Ronan hops in the driver's seat and Mac in the passenger seat. Patty cradles my head while Finn kneels, squished between the seats, getting to work. Ronan peels out of the docking bay and pulls out on the main drive.

"Where do I go? We can't go to the cops; we can't go to a fucking hospital, and in his condition, we can't go to an airport. I need options" He slams his hand on the steering wheel.

Turning the phone on, I scroll through the list of recent calls till I find the number and hit call. It rings a few times till a man picks it up

"Miss Gorbachev didn't expect to hear from you so soon. Calling in that favor already?" A thick Italian accent comes through the phone.

197

"My name is Liam O'Conner; Anya is in trouble; I need your help."

"You have it. I owe her. What do you need?"

"First, I need to find a way out of Vegas, and then I need help going to war."

"How do you feel about New York, Mr. O' Conner."

"Bloody delightful," I grit out.

Finn gives me something for the pain, and before I fade into darkness, I make a vow.

I'm coming for you, love, and I will burn Sin City to the ground or die trying. Saving Baba Yaga is my only mission.

So begins the war...

Follow me

Instagram: author_s.j_magnolia
TikTok: magnoliarustic82

Acknowledgments

I'm not sure where to start, but to be honest, I have a lot of people to thank for getting me here. My family should always come first. My children will probably never read this book lol but cheered me on the whole way anyway.

My love, you inspired who Liam is at his core. Loyal to a fault, brutally honest, and loves his woman fiercely even if she doesn't deserve it sometimes. Thank you for pushing and bragging me up to anyone who would listen.

I wouldn't have made it this far without the support, encouragement, and criticism which I mean in the best way from my friends. Katie, Michelle, Willow, Jackie, and Monica, you amazing women held me together through this, gave me sound advice, hard lessons when I needed to hear them, laughs, tears, and everything in between.

Jeanine, my amazing editor, you are an absolute godsend, you took such amazing care with my book baby, made it brilliant, and helped me learn how to become a better writer. I have learned some immense lessons writing this book and although hard to hear sometimes ultimately made me better and more willing to learn. It's no easy feat to write a book and I'm still processing I'm here at this stage.

I would also like to give a shout-out to Jessica and the

Self Pub Hub community for giving me a space to learn from other authors, meet people I now call friends, and a safe space to be unapologetically myself. I'm looking forward to the next step and I hope everyone enjoys Anya's story as much as I loved writing it. Thank you from the bottom of my heart.

S.J x

About the Author

Sarah Jane has always dreamt of being a writer. It wasn't until covid hit and she was faced with a diagnosis of Lupus and Inflammatory arthritis that she finally decided to make that dream a reality. The biggest lesson she has learned adjusting to life with this disease and during this process is to be selfish with your time, it's fleeting so do the things that bring you joy, worry less, and make as many memories as possible. When she's not writing S.J. can be found hiking with friends, reading books from her mini-library at home, taking photographs of old buildings, with her kids on an adventure, and doing anything else she sets her mind to. Sarah resides in Alberta, Canada with her family and two dogs Anya and Cooper.

Manufactured by Amazon.ca
Bolton, ON